FIRST LICKS

"You are Golden Hawk," the Blackfoot said, and spat in Hawk's face.

Hawk reached for his Bowie. But before he could grab it, hands grabbed him from behind. He was held helpless as he was savagely beaten, then slammed dazed to the ground.

The Blackfoot stepped close to Hawk. Sizing him up carefully, the Indian kicked Hawk in the groin. As the pain exploded through Hawk's gut clear to his back teeth, the Blackfoot leaned his face close to Hawk's.

"You one fine prize for Johnny Bear," he told Hawk, then moved back a step, and this time carefully kicked Hawk in the face, the tip of his boot catching Hawk under his right cheek bone with enough force to flip him over backward.

And there was nothing for Hawk to do but take it—until it was his turn to pay it back with interest. . . .

GOLDEN HAWK #9

THE SEARCHERS

Will C. Knott

A SIGNET BOOK

NEW AMERICAN LIBRARY

PUBLISHER'S NOTE

This book is a work of fiction. Names, characters, places, and incidents either are the product of the author's imagination or are used fictitiously, and any resemblance to actual persons, living or dead, events, or locales is entirely coincidental.

NAL BOOKS ARE AVAILABLE AT QUANTITY DISCOUNTS WHEN USED TO PROMOTE PRODUCTS OR SERVICES. FOR INFORMATION PLEASE WRITE TO PREMIUM MARKETING DIVISION, NEW AMERICAN LIBRARY, 1633 BROADWAY, NEW YORK, NEW YORK 10019.

SIGNET TRADEMARK REG. U.S. PAT. OFF. AND FOREIGN COUNTRIES
REGISTERED TRADEMARK—MARCA REGISTRADA
HECHO EN CHICAGO, U.S.A.

SIGNET, SIGNET CLASSIC, MENTOR, ONYX, PLUME, MERIDIAN and NAL BOOKS are published by NAL PENGUIN INC., 1633 Broadway, New York, New York 10019

First Printing, September, 1988

1 2 3 4 5 6 7 8 9

PRINTED IN THE UNITED STATES OF AMERICA

GOLDEN HAWK

A quiet stream under the Comanche moon ...
leaping savages ... knives flashing in the firelight
... brutal, shameful death ...

Ripped from the bosom of their slain parents and
carried off by the raiding Comanches, Jed Thompson and his sister can never forget that hellish
night under the glare of the Comanche moon, seared
into their memories forever.

Years later, his vengeance slaked, pursued relentlessly by his past Comanche brothers, Jed is now
Golden Hawk. Half Comanche, half white man. A
legend in his time, an awesome nemesis to some—a
bulwark and a refuge to any man or woman lost in
the terror of that raw, savage land.

—1—

Hawk ducked his head into the icy spring and held it under the frigid cataract for almost thirty seconds. When he flung his head up out of it, shaking his massive mane of golden hair, he was blowing like a grizzly who had just missed a trout.

Despite the chill mountain air, he had thrown off his deerskin shirt, revealing muscles that stood out like mole tunnels. Pulling away from the spring, he rested back on his haunches and gazed alertly about like any other wild beast of the wilderness, his sharp, commanding sky-blue eyes resembling those of an eagle perched on some lofty crag.

Satisfied he was alone, that no Blackfoot or long-traveling Comanche had followed him into Oregon Territory, Hawk got to his full six feet two, combed the moisture out of his unruly mop of hair with long, powerful fingers. Then he bent and plucked his buckskin shirt off the ground beside him, tossed it on, and buttoned it up, his massive shoulders filling it out impressively.

He strode back to the stream-fed meadow where he had hobbled his black. He saddled it, then rolled up his sleeping blanket and tied it securely behind

7

the cantle. He worked swiftly, anxious to be on his way. He had had a good night's sleep and was hungry, but he had decided to save for a more desperate time his few remaining strings of jerky. Tames Horses' band was only a few miles farther on and he expected to dine with the old chief on fresh venison if not buffalo in celebration of his arrival.

He was about to swing into his saddle when he heard sudden, piercing screams coming from just beyond a wooded ridge farther downstream. The screams filled the morning wilderness with terror and Hawk found himself on the move even before he consciously willed it. Pulling his huge Walker Colt from his belt, he ran swiftly to the ridge and plunged into the pines crowning it.

Breaking out of the timber a moment later, he saw below him the stream looping back around the ridge and a grassy bank shaded by alders crowding close upon it. On the bank two Indian women were fighting off two white men. The women had come to the stream to bathe and had been caught as naked as on the day God made them, their deerskin dresses piled neatly on a grassy sward under the alders. They were considerably smaller than their burly attackers, but were putting up a fierce struggle—so fierce they were no longer wasting any more energy screaming, while their white attackers were experiencing much difficulty peeling off their britches and at the same time holding on to their thrashing victims.

Keeping to the ridge, Hawk worked his way around behind the struggling figures. Then he angled down the steep slope behind them until he was within a few yards. The larger of the two men had managed to discard his britches and had cuffed the Indian woman under him into sullen submission. The other white man was not so far along and was being beaten back steadily by the furious woman twisting and gyrating wildly under him.

Both women caught glimpses of Hawk's stealthy approach, but did nothing to betray him. Pulling up behind the fellow with his britches off, Hawk brought the barrel of the Walker Colt down on the back of the attacker's head, taking some care not to strike with all his strength. If he had, the heavy Walker would have crushed the white man's skull like an eggshell. As it was, he sagged to the ground without a sound.

The other white man was already turning to deal with Hawk. Hawk thumb-cocked and aimed the Colt and fired coolly. At that distance the detonation alone was enough to shatter the man's composure. When the smoke cleared, Hawk saw the raw crease left by the ball, starting at the man's cheekbone and carrying away with it most of his left ear. With a startled screech of agony, the man clapped his hand over the bloody stump and spun away from Hawk. Hawk stepped closer and finished him off with a single chopping stroke of his Walker. The man's screeching stopped abruptly and he crumpled to the ground.

Hawk turned to the two Indian women. One glance at their sleek hair, their bronzed, high cheekbones, and their slightly canted, almond-shaped eyes, and he knew them to be Nez Percé. They were both about the same age, he guessed, not more than sixteen or seventeen, probably already married and in the first full bloom of their young womanhood. The sight of them had been too much of a temptation for the two white men.

Hawk had picked up enough of the Nez Percé tongue to ask the two maidens, now hastily knotting the drawstrings on their shiftlike dresses, where they were from.

They pointed upstream.

"Of what band are you?"

"The Yellow Grass band," the taller of the two women responded.

Hawk smiled. This was Tames Horses' band. They had moved farther westward than any other Nez Percé band to escape the constantly marauding Blackfoot, and had indeed found a lovely country. The only question that remained was whether they could keep it from the settlers now pouring into Oregon in such numbers.

"I will return with you to your camp," Hawk told them.

They smiled, perfectly willing to have Hawk accompany them.

The smiles froze on their faces.

Hawk spun.

Three armed men on horseback were breaking from the timber downstream and were heading toward them at a fast gallop. It was clear the two men Hawk had dealt with a moment before had ties with this group. As the three riders charged toward them, one fired his rifle. The ball slammed into the ground a few yards in front of Hawk.

He spoke to the women. "Go back to your village! Hurry!"

The women needed no urging. As they raced

upstream, Hawk ducked toward the timber leading to the ridge, in order to draw the three horsemen after him. He had almost reached the trees when one of the riders overtook him and flung himself from his horse, landing on Hawk's back. He was a big man and his crushing weight bore Hawk to the ground. But he rolled out of the man's grasp, kicked him in the crotch, broke once more for the timber, and reached it ahead of the other two. Hawk raced up the slope to the ridge and dashed through the pines, the three men pushing their mounts up through the tangle of brush and timber after him.

Once out of the pines, Hawk raced down the side of the ridge and flung himself onto his black, pulling his Hawken from its boot. He got off one shot, catching the lead pursuer's horse in the chest. As it went down, throwing its rider, the other two swerved around it. Hawk exchanged revolver shots with them, then spurred his black down a grassy slope ... and suddenly found himself surrounded by five, then six riders, all of them armed.

Hawk pulled his mount to a halt and prudently stuck his revolver into his belt as the riders slowly circled him, looking him over the way a butcher would a side of beef on a hook.

One of the two pursuing riders, his face almost completely hidden by a thick beard, pulled alongside him. "Who the hell might you be, mister?"

Hawk said nothing.

"We ain't goin' to kill you," Blackbeard said. "We'll leave that to our two pardners back there—less'n you killed them both. In that case, we'll just chop you up for our camp dogs." He grinned, revealing surprisingly white teeth.

Another rider—a thin redhead wearing a black wool stocking cap—hauled his horse around and, reaching over, deftly lifted Hawk's Walker Colt from his belt and stuck it into his own.

"You one of them no-account mountain men we hear tell about?" he snickered and wiped his nose with the back of his hand. "Guess maybe you is. You smell worse'n a grizzly in heat."

A third rider pulled up on the other side of Hawk. This rider, wearing a black, floppy-brimmed hat, a red-checked woolen shirt, and greasy buckskin britches, had eyes as jet-black as his thick, braided hair. He was a Blackfoot, something Hawk knew at once, not only from his cheekbones and the slant of his forehead, but from the stiff-backed, splay-legged manner in which he rode.

And then of course there were the black moccasins.

"You are Golden Hawk," the Blackfoot said.

Hawk did not bother to respond.

The Blackfoot spat in his face.

Hawk threw himself at him. With his hands closing about the Indian's neck, he bore him backward off his horse. The Indian struck the ground before Hawk. As his breath exploded from his lungs, the Blackfoot grunted painfully. He was dazed. Hawk reached for his bowie. But before he could grab it, he was pulled off the Indian and hauled upright, his knife snatched from its sheath.

With his arms held behind him, by two of the men, the others took turns punishing Hawk with their boots and fists until he swayed drunkenly in their grasp, his head hanging, his senses reeling. Satisfied, the men released him and stepped back, letting him slam forward into the ground. Hawk was only dimly aware of the Blackfoot stepping close to him. Sizing him up carefully, the Indian kicked Hawk in the groin. As the pain exploded up through his gut, past his solar plexus clear to his back teeth, the Blackfoot leaned his face close to Hawk's.

"You one fine prize for Johnny Bear," he told Hawk. "I sell you to Blackfoot chief for many horses—and maybe his daughter."

Johnny Bear smiled then and stood up, moved aside a few steps, and this time kicked Hawk carefully in the face, the tip of his boot catching Hawk under his right cheekbone with enough force to flip him over backward.

Into darkness.

"Mister! Hey, mister, wake up!"

Hawk opened his eyes. He was lying prone on the bed of a wagon. From under him came the jolting creak and rumble of iron-shod wheels rolling over uneven ground. The right side of his face was so swollen, he could see only out of his left eye.

Turning his head, he saw a boy of sixteen or so leaning over him, his eyes anxious. Beyond him, Hawk saw, was a young woman sprawled on the other side of the wagon bed, her ripped skirt and torn bodice barely covering her. She was unconscious, her head resting facedown on her crossed arms, her long blond hair spilling over the wagon's bed.

Hawk pushed himself to a sitting position, not an easy task, since his wrists had been bound tightly by rawhide strips.

"Who are you?" Hawk asked the boy.

"Sam. Sam Baldwin."

"Who's that woman over there?"

"My sister. Her name's Marta."

"Where are they taking us?"

"Back to the fort."

"Fort Emory?"

"Yes."

"What the hell is going on here?"

"Bannister and his men have taken over the fort."

"Taken it over? How could that be? What happened to the chief factor?"

"You mean MacDuff?"

"Yes."

"Bannister killed him—and the other traders, too."

This was difficult to believe. But the boy spoke with such calm matter-of-factness that Hawk could not doubt him. "This man Bannister . . . is he the one with the beard covering his face?"

"That's him, all right. They call him Judge."

"What the hell's he up to, anyway?"

"He wants to take over the fur trade in these mountains, then deal directly to the ships captains, the ones working the China trade. They can sell the furs when they get East and make a pile of money. Bannister's working with the ship captains. And he's payin' the Indian trappers better than the other traders."

"Better than the American Fur Company."

"That's what I heard. But I couldn't say for sure. I don't know what them traders give the Indians for pelts."

"It ain't much. It never is. The blankets are thin and the rum ain't fit for a hog to drink. But I can't imagine this Bannister doing any better."

"The thing is, he's sidin' with the Blackfoot against the Nez Percé. That's what I hear, anyway."

"And so the Blackfoot will let his trappers into their hunting ground."

Sam nodded.

"And now Fort Emory is Bannister's base."

"Yes."

"These wagons we're in now. Where'd they come from? Do they belong to Bannister?"

"No. They're what's left of a Quaker wagon train headin' into Oregon." The boy frowned unhappily. "I guess I'm the one responsible. I led Bannister's men right to them."

"Go slow, boy. I'm havin' trouble following you."

"Marta and I escaped from Bannister, and when we came on this wagon train, the settlers and the Quakers took us in and fed us and all—only they wouldn't believe it when we told them what Bannister was up to. Said we was out of our heads. The next day Bannister's men attacked the wagon train for their goods. Most of the men were taken alive. They're in the other wagons behind us."

"What about the women?"

"Them and the children were given to the Blackfoot for their help."

It took a while for Hawk to digest such grim news. When he had, he thought of something else that puzzled him.

"Sam, you say you escaped from Bannister. That he followed you. Why? What's so valuable about a young lad like yourself and his sister?"

Sam moistened his lips unhappily. "It ain't me Bannister wants. It's Marta."

"Why?"

"Bannister figures he can sell her."

"Sell her?"

"That's right. To the captain of one of the ships he brings the furs to . . . and then the captain will sell Marta to some Arabs who buy white women for their harems."

Sam looked away from Hawk. Speaking of what might be in store for his sister was destroying his composure.

"That's okay," Hawk told him gently. "You don't have to talk about it if you don't want to."

"I'm all right," Sam said, blinking back his tears.

"You're certain that's what Bannister plans to do?"

"I overheard him. He was tellin' his men to stay away from Marta. He said he didn't want her spoiled. That way the captain could get a better price from some sultan he knows."

Hawk glanced over at Marta. Almost as if she had become aware she was the subject of their conversation, she stirred slightly and groaned, then pushed her head and shoulders off the bed, staring blankly at Hawk, then turning her gaze on her brother. There was a welt on the side of her forehead only partially hidden by the spill of her long blond hair.

Sam asked her how she was. In a weak voice she told him she was fine. Then Sam introduced her to Hawk. She nodded dazedly at Hawk, then settled herself back down onto the wagon bed, evidently completely exhausted and dispirited by her ordeal. Nevertheless, Hawk noted, she had not uttered a single word of complaint.

Hawk leaned back against the wagon's canvas.

The rough journey over the stony, uneven ground was a constant trial. It was difficult for him to digest all of what Sam had just told him.

During his short visit to his sister back East a couple of years before, Hawk had often visited the Boston port to watch the great merchant ships arrive from the Far East and China, their huge sails billowing like clouds. Mingling with the sailors and longshoremen, he had heard many strange tales of China and India and of the Muslim rulers of the Middle East and North Africa as well—especially their unquenchable appetite for white women, for whom, it was said, they would pay truly fabulous prices.

What Sam was telling him then did not seem at all unlikely.

Furthermore, Hawk had been hearing of strange bands of adventurers from the West Coast doing their best to cut into the fur trade with the aid and encouragement of clipper ship captains. This man Bannister was evidently one such adventurer. He wouldn't last long, Hawk was sure. The tribes in these mountains would not stand still for the kind of tactics he employed, no matter how much better the goods he offered in trade might be. But for the moment at least, Bannister was capable of causing considerable mischief, especially with the Blackfoot as his willing accomplices.

"Help me get free," Hawk told Sam.

The boy held up his hands. They were mannacled, the chains fastened to the wagon bed with metal cleats. He could not reach Hawk unless Hawk moved closer. Hawk worked himself over to Sam.

"There's a knife in a sheath at the back of my

neck," he told Sam. "Use it to cut the knot in this rawhide."

Sam's iron manacles chinked against the side of Hawk's head as the boy worked the knife from its sheath. Pulling back, Hawk held out his wrists. As soon as the boy cut through the knot, Hawk used his teeth to unwind the rawhide, then leaned forward to allow Sam to replace the throwing knife behind his neck.

Hawk glanced out through the front hole in the canvas and saw the head and shoulders of the wagon's driver. He looked out the rear and caught fleeting glimpses of his captors riding alongside as they escorted the wagons. One of the riders had a bloody bandanna wrapped around his head. This was probably the worthy fellow whose ear Hawk had blown off.

Hawk looked at the boy. "How far are we from the fort, would you say?"

"We should be there soon."

Hawk stuck his hands out again, his wrists held close together. "Quick. Wind the rawhide back around my wrists. But not tightly. Then tuck the end under so it won't hang."

Sam did as Hawk told him. As Sam was finishing up, Hawk glanced out past the driver and saw the fort's palisaded ramparts looming just ahead. He pushed himself away from Sam, and by the time the wagon entered the fort a few moments later, he was lying prone, his apparently securely bound wrists held in close to his stomach.

— 2 —

His eyes still closed, Hawk heard the heavy footsteps of Bannister's men as they clambered into the
rear of the wagon. He did not look up as he heard
the shackles being pulled free of the wagon floor
and the muffled cries as Sam and his sister were
dragged from the wagon and dumped onto the
ground.

Then another, lighter pair of footsteps approached
Hawk and he smelled Johnny Bear looming over
him. The Indian's rough claw of a hand closed
about Hawk's shoulder and yanked him up and
around so sharply that the back of his head slammed
against the wagon's high wooden side.

Hawk allowed his eyes to flicker open.

Johnny Bear—his face a mask of savage triumph—
leaned close. "Huh, Golden Hawk!" he cried, his
anthracite eyes gleaming with happy malice. "Why
you not fly from here? Is this not the Great Canni-
bal Owl?"

Hawk stared calmly back at the Indian.

"Speak, Great Warrior! Unless your fear is too
great. If it is, I will understand."

Hawk cleared his throat and spat in the Blackfoot's face.

The Indian straightened up, wiping his face furiously. Then he moved quickly forward and kicked Hawk in the chest. Hawk rolled over and tucked himself up into a ball in a prudent effort to protect his vitals from the Blackfoot's fury. He was only slightly successful as the Indian proceeded to work Hawk over with a careful, deliberate thoroughness until he had worn himself out completely. Then he grabbed Hawk by the hair, hauled him upright, and with a well-placed kick sent him sailing out of the back of the wagon.

Hawk turned himself slightly in midair so that he landed on his side and was able to roll over onto his feet. A few of Bannister's men who were not occupied in marching the rest of the captives off toward a warehouse applauded with roars of laughter Hawk's agility in regaining his feet, but their cries did not please Johnny Bear at all. He jumped down from the wagon and grabbed Hawk by the hair, then flung him toward the palisade's inner wall. Hawk managed to stay on his feet, but after receiving two more brutal shoves, Hawk slammed headlong into the wooden fence. With a contemptuous snort, the Blackfoot kicked Hawk's feet out from under him. Hawk crashed to the ground, his back smacking against the wall.

"I will be back, White Pig," Johnny Bear snarled down at him. "Soon we ride out to my people. It is long ride. It will not be easy for the great Golden Hawk!"

Satisfied that Hawk would not be going anywhere,

the Indian strode off. Watching him go, Hawk was perfectly content. Johnny Bear was right. Hawk would still be here when the Indian returned, and not much later, as soon as they put this fort behind them, Hawk would even the score.

Johnny Bear rode through the timber, his attention on the trail ahead. Hawk trudged alongside, the Blackfoot's two packhorses following behind them on a rawhide lead tied to the Indian's saddle. Johnny Bear had dropped the loop of his reata over Hawk's neck and now held the rope loosely in his hand. When the mood came on him, he would yank Hawk forward with cruel suddenness, sometimes spilling Hawk forward onto his knees. At such times the Blackfoot could hardly contain his savage joy at having the great Golden Hawk under his thumb. They were three hours away from the fort and they had about an hour of daylight left, Hawk figured.

Johnny Bear was astride Hawk's black and was using Hawk's saddle. He had decided to make himself a gift of Hawk's hat, rifle, Walker Colt, and bowie knife as well. He hadn't made any effort yet to appropriate Hawk's scalp, preferring instead to exhibit the man with his head intact when he rode into his village with Hawk on a leash.

They broke out of the timber. Ahead was a gentle slope and beyond that a wide stream. On the far side of the stream a few small bunches of buffalo were grazing. At the sight of the buffalo, Johnny Bear came alert. Hawk could tell the Blackfoot was trying to decide whether to go after one of the cows or to continue on with Hawk without pause.

Hawk chose to make the decision for him.

While Johnny Bear's attention was riveted on the buffalo, Hawk lifted his bound wrists to his mouth. With his teeth he pulled loose the end Sam Baldwin had tucked under and then with a few quick tugs loosened the rawhide enough to enable him to pull his wrists free. He reached up and lifted the noose over his head. Johnny Bear caught the movement of the rawhide and swiveled to look at Hawk.

Hawk yanked hard on the reata. The rawhide was looped around the Blackfoot's wrist, and before he could free himself, he was dragged off the saddle. Even as the Indian hit the ground, Hawk was reaching back for his throwing knife. The Blackfoot sat up clumsily, his dark face twisted in fury. Hawk waited. Johnny Bear jumped up and clawed for the Colt. Hawk let his knife fly. The blade twinkled in the late-afternoon sunlight like something alive a second before its blade sank into the Blackfoot's neck just below his Adam's apple.

Dropping the Colt, Johnny Bear reached up and yanked the blade out of his neck, a sudden red spray of blood bursting out after it, the blood pouring down his chest and puddling under him. He looked down in terrified amazement at the steady stream of his life's blood flowing from him, then sank onto his knees and sat down hard. Hawk walked over and took the blade from the Indian's hand, then picked his Colt up off the ground. Silently, eyes wide in pure astonishment at this sudden reversal of fortune, Johnny Bear stared at Hawk, blood now dribbling out of the corners of his mouth. Hawk put his foot on the Blackfoot's shoulder and shoved him firmly back. The Blackfoot slammed back onto the ground, his head striking the dirt hard, Hawk's wide-brimmed hat rolling free.

Hawk bent down to look more closely at the Indian and saw that Johnny Bear was no longer staring up at him . . . or at anything in this universe.

He picked up his hat and proceeded to reclaim his black and the rest of his gear. He figured that if he started back to the fort immediately he should reach it after dark.

It was a little past midnight and the moon was keeping out of sight behind a milky bank of clouds. The gateway to the fort, Hawk had already noted, was guarded by only one white man. Hawk approached him carefully, keeping to the shadows cast by the fort's high wall. The guard appeared to be asleep on his feet, his hands clasping the top of his rifle barrel. He was snoring slightly. As Hawk leaned close to take the rifle from him, he became aware of the awesome stench of rotgut that hovered about the man. He was dead-drunk.

Hawk slipped the man's knife from its sheath and took his sack of lead balls and his powder horn. As he lifted the powder horn's leather loop over the man's head, the fellow came awake and started to mumble something. Hawk clubbed him on the side of the head with the barrel of his Colt. The fellow slumped soundlessly to the ground.

Hawk slung the powder horn over his shoulder, then propped the unconscious man's back up against the fort's outer wall beside the gate, so that anyone looking out to check on him would simply assume he had sat down to rest and had fallen asleep.

Carrying the guard's rifle as well as his own in the crook of his left arm and holding his bowie knife in his right hand, Hawk slipped into the fort and stayed in the shadows close under the wall. He came eventually to the stables and paused outside the open door, listening to the sound of the horses stamping and blowing in their stalls. There didn't seem to be any stable boy on guard, so he ducked past the door. In the corral beyond the stable, mules and packhorses were bunched in opposite corners, swishing their tails and nodding their heads nervously, sensing Hawk's presence as he glided past them.

Hawk approached what appeared to be the main living quarters, a series of four long rooms, constructed of rough logs and built hard against the fort's northern wall. Hawk heard the voices of Bannister's men coming from inside the closest room. Slipping past it, he glanced through a side window and saw Bannister's men crowding around a poker table. One of them, grinning widely, was reaching for the pot. Bannister was not in sight. It looked like there were seven men in the room, at least.

Hawk moved on and was passing a bunkhouse when its door swung open. A Bannock appeared in the doorway, blinking in the dark at Hawk's tall, powerful figure. A whiskey jug dangled from his right hand. The Bannock opened his mouth to cry out, but Hawk slit his throat and stepped back as the Indian toppled forward through the doorway.

Swiftly, Hawk leaned his two rifles against the bunkhouse wall, then took the dead Bannock by the hair, dragged him into the bunkhouse and across the dirt floor to an empty bunk, and dumped him onto it facedown. The only light in the place came from a dim candle on a table in the far corner. A second Bannock was slumped facedown onto the table, snoring. A whiskey jug rested beside his cheek. Hawk considered the sleeping figure a moment to make sure he wasn't playing possum. He walked over, picked up the whiskey jug, and broke it over the Indian's skull. Then he left the bunkhouse, picked up his rifles, and went on.

A moment later the fort's fur warehouse materialized out of the shadows ahead of him. On the ground beside its double doors sat another Bannock, his head hanging over the neck of a whiskey jug resting on his crossed legs. His flintlock rifle was propped against the warehouse's rough log wall beside him.

Moving stealthily closer, Hawk leaned his rifles against the warehouse wall, snatched the Bannock's flintlock by the barrel, and swung the stock like a sledgehammer, catching the Indian on the side of his head. The Indian sprawled lengthwise and lay still, his jug spinning along the ground into the darkness.

Lifting the beam that lay across the wide double doors, Hawk pulled one of them open and peered inside. He heard a faint movement in the darkness and with it came the smell of cooped-up humans . . . and of something far worse. Lugging three rifles by this time, he stepped into the warehouse and pulled the door shut. Moonlight filtered through dirt-encrusted loft windows high above. It was the only source of light, but gradually his eyes grew accustomed to the nearly impenetrable darkness, and he was able to make out the figures bunched in a corner to his right. The stench did not come from them, he realized, but from the other end of the warehouse.

"Sam," Hawk called softly. "Sam Baldwin! You in here?"

"Who're you?" a shadowy figure called.

"I'm looking for Sam and his sister, Marta," Hawk replied.

"They're on the way to the coast. Bannister and his sidekicks took them with them—along with a couple of wagon loads of prime fur."

A match flared as someone lit a candle and placed it on a beam behind the prisoners. The relief to Hawk's eyes was welcome as he walked toward the fellow who had answered him. He was an angular gent with a neatly trimmed beard and glowing black eyes set in deep hollows.

"What're you doin' here, mister?"

"What's it look like? I've come to help you get out of here."

"I figured that. I'm only askin' because the last time I saw you, you was bein' hauled off by that no-account Blackfoot."

"I figured maybe it wouldn't be a good idea for me to go home with him."

"Where is he now?"

"With his ancestors in the Sand Hills. What's your name, mister?"

"Tim Holcolm," the fellow said, shaking Hawk's hand. "What's yours?"

"Jed Thompson."

One of the prisoners said, "I heard that Indian calling you Hawk."

"There's some that do call me that," Hawk acknowledged.

The rest of the prisoners crowded around to shake his hand. In the candle's flickering light Hawk could see their drawn, haggard faces, their haunted eyes staring out of deep sockets. It was clear they had been through a miserable ordeal, but now, with Hawk's unexpected arrival, hope lit their gaunt faces.

"Which of you are the Quakers?" Hawk asked them.

Four men raised their hands.

"You don't have to take part in this breakout if you don't want to," he told them. "There's going to be some bloodshed, that's for sure. So just keep back and let the rest of us handle it."

A white-bearded Quaker, no more than five and a half feet tall, but with broad, impressive shoulders, spoke up. "Just give me one of them rifles, Jed. I was a man before I was a Quaker. These devils are going to pay for takin' my wife."

A quick mutter of agreement swept through the others. Not a single one of them—including the Quakers—was willing to sit this one out. They all had scores to settle, it seemed.

"What's your name?" Hawk asked the white-bearded Quaker.

"Caleb Tribe."

Hawk handed him one of the rifles he had been carrying and gave another one to Tim Holcolm, keeping his own Hawken for himself. Then he passed them the powder horn and ball pouch.

As the two men saw to their priming, Hawk

glanced at the other end of the warehouse. "What's causing that stench over there?"

Holcolm looked up from the rifle. "Them's the corpses of the traders and the factor that was here when Bannister and his men arrived. They didn't even bother to bury the bodies. Half of them are mutilated and most have lost their scalps, not to mention their nuts."

"Bannocks?"

"Yep. They helped some. But from what I hear, Bannister's men weren't at all bashful about joinin' in."

Hawk was sickened. He had met the chief factor MacDuff briefly a year ago before the ruddy Scotsman had headed out of Fort Hall to set up this trading post, and he had liked him from the moment he met him.

"You got a plan, Jed?" Caleb Tribe asked, resting his loaded and primed rifle on his shoulder.

"Any hay up in that loft?"

"There's plenty," said one of the men.

"Throw down as much as you can and pile most of it on those bodies over there. Then light it and follow the three of us out of here. Keep your heads down when you come. There's liable to be plenty of lead flying."

Thanks to the complacency of their captors, none of the men was shackled. As most of them clambered up the ladders to the loft, Hawk pushed open the door carefully and peered out. The way looked clear. He could hear dimly the sound of Bannister's men. They were still gambling and sounded much louder, which meant they were more drunk than they had been when he slipped past their quarters. Fine. The rotgut whiskey churning in their guts would raise hell with their judgment.

"What's in that building over there?" Hawk asked Holcolm, pointing to a blockhouselike structure about twenty yards away sitting in the center of the fort's quadrangle.

"That was the sutler's store and the trading post—or it was before Bannister got here."

"We'll use it for cover," Hawk said. "When Bannister's men come running to put out the fire, we'll open up on them from there."

"With only three rifles?" Caleb asked.

"Don't forget this cannon," Hawk reminded him, slapping the Walker Colt stuck in his belt.

Hawk pushed the door open all the way and led the two men swiftly across the yard to the building. Crouching down in its shadow, Hawk waved Holcolm and Tribe farther down the length of the building, then stretched out flat on the ground to wait. From this vantage point he could watch the quarters holding Bannister's men. Raucous laughter was erupting from the building almost constantly. A door opened and a man too drunk to stand spilled out, then sprawled facedown on the ground. Once he hit it, he did not stir again.

Hawk squinted at the warehouse, waiting.

The fire had been lit. He could see that much. Smoke was pouring out from around the double doors. "They'd better get out of there," Hawk muttered aloud to Tribe.

"That's what I was thinkin'," Tribe called out softly, sounding as nervous as Hawk.

"Here they come," cried Holcolm.

The double doors swung wide as the rest of the prisoners poured out, racing full tilt toward them. As they reached the corner of the blockhouse where Hawk lay, he waved them around behind the building.

"Keep your asses down," he told them as they ran past.

They vanished into the darkness behind the store. Hawk glanced back at the warehouse. There were no flames yet, but waves of smoke were billowing out through the open doorway like a black, silent surf. From inside the warehouse came a sudden gleam, then a wink of light, followed by a deep, powerful detonation. The black smoke vanished and in its place a thick tongue of fire lanced out through the doorway. The entire warehouse shuddered. Instantly, flames were climbing up its outside walls. The loft windows began to glow like satanic eyes.

Hawk cupped his hand to his mouth. "Fire," he cried. "The warehouse is on fire!"

Hawk heard a table turn over and shouts, and a second later Bannister's men piled out of their quarters into the night. From other corners of the fort came a few Indians. Bannocks. As the shouting, astonished crowd rushed toward the warehouse, the flames broke through the loft, sending a garish glow over the approaching men. They had no buckets, no way to quench the flames, but they came on anyway, drawn like moths to the awesome, quaking fire that was rapidly turning night into day.

One fellow in a stocking cap and a ragged deerskin jacket stared up in appalled entrancement at the flames. He held a whiskey jug in his hand. Jed lifted his Hawken and took him out with a single shot. Dumping a fresh load of powder into the barrel, he spat a ball into it, slammed the butt gently on the ground to seat it, and took out a Bannock at the rear of the crowd. Farther down, Holcolm and Tribe began to pour a steady, murderous hail of fire into the demoralized, milling gang, reloading their weapons with the speed and enthusiasm of demons pouring flames into hell.

Caught as they were in the fire's brilliant light, Bannister's men made excellent targets. Few of Hawk's rounds—or those of his two companions—seemed to miss. Men were dropping everywhere. The result was wild confusion, then sheer panic as Hawk took out his Walker and pumped an even more rapid stream of fire into their midst. Completely bewildered, the men staggered blindly about, with only three or four making any attempt to return the fire.

But since they had no idea who was attacking and no clear sense of where the attack was coming from, they gave up and broke for the fort's gate. At once, Hawk and his two companions leapt to their feet and took after them, maintaining all the while a steady, withering fire and managing to bring down three more. Only five made it out through the gate, and two of those, Hawk noted, were Bannocks.

Reaching the gate, Hawk pulled up and searched the inky blackness. He could hear the men crashing blindly through the night. Without weapons or a mount in this wilderness, Hawk thought with some satisfaction, a man was as helpless as an exposed infant. Bannister's men were finished as a threat.

He turned around, carefully reloaded his Walker, and returned with Holcolm and Tribe to the killing ground. It was a horror, the dark earth alive with the twisting, writhing bodies of those who had been cut down. Their cries filled the night. Hawk and his two companions—one of them a Quaker—had turned this fort into a corner of hell.

But all Hawk needed to steel himself against the horror was the memory of that stinking pile of multilated bodies they had just cremated.

It was the next day. The warehouse had been allowed to burn to the ground, its flames confined to that side of the fort. A portion of the palisades had been lost as well, leaving a great black gap, but the damage was not beyond repair if the fur company was all that anxious to send out another factor.

The dead were buried in a mass grave behind the fort, the wounded remnants of Bannister's band groaning or suffering silently in their bunks. No one had thought to tend them. And no one worried about it, either. They had other brands in the fire. At the moment the men were lining up just inside the gate, getting ready to move out. Some had saddled the horses that had been left behind by Bannister, the remainder were prepared to march on foot.

The night before they had made their decision. Not a man among them was going on to the Willamette Valley, not without their women and children. With Hawk to lead them, they were determined to overtake Bannister's Blackfoot allies and get back their people . . . or die in the attempt, an outcome that did not seem all that unlikely to Hawk, considering the settlers' woeful inexperience in such matters. This awareness did not make him any less willing to guide them, however.

Hawk was astride his black, looking over the motley crew he would be guiding into Blackfoot country, when one of the Quakers ran through the gate toward them.

"Indians!" he cried.

To every man there that meant Blackfoot, and most of the men began looking to their priming, while others rushed about aimlessly. Hawk told them all to stay where they were and rode up to the running man.

"Where are they?" he asked him.

Pulling up hastily, the fellow pointed back out through the gate. "On the other side of the meadow," he cried.

"How many?"

"I just saw two—but there's more!"

"You're probably right. Get over there with the others."

Hawk urged his horse into a lope and rode out through the gate into the wide clearing that encircled the fort. Scanning the far edge of the meadow, Hawk saw a small force of mounted Indians breaking from the timber. He relaxed at once. From the look of their feathered lances and bonnets, and especially from the way their war ponies were bedecked, he knew at once they were not Blackfoot, but friendly Nez Percé.

He spurred toward them and soon recognized one of the Nez Percé in the forefront of the party. Tames Horses. Elated, he waved to the old warrior and pulled up.

Tames Horses left the chief behind as he rode out ahead to greet Hawk. When he pulled up alongside Hawk, he was unable to contain his delight at seeing his old friend again. His wrinkled map of a face screwed into a pleased grin.

"You old buzzard," Hawk growled in the warrior's tongue. "This child's heart soars. Been looking all over for you."

"I am back with my people," Tames Horses replied proudly. "You see? I no longer sit in the quiet forest and wait for the grizzly to find me."

"You're a young man again."

"A certain part of me is young again," he said, his black-button eyes twinkling. "Though I have found the breasts of woman still as hard as stone, their bellies are soft—and this old chief is content."

"Glad to hear it, Tames Horses. But my people got trouble. Some men back there in the fort lost their women and children to the Blackfoot, and the fort's chief factor has been killed."

"We know of this. We are sad when we heard the bearded white man kill the old trader, the one who blow the sad pipes. This bearded white man say to our people he trade much fine goods for our furs. Maybe so. But he and his men are iron hearts. The Nez Percé will not bring their pelts to him. This place stink of death. Only the filthy Bannock and the treacherous Blackfoot bring their furs here."

Hawk nodded grimly. "I should've figured you'd be knowing what's going on."

"We see fire last night. It lights the sky. I say it is Golden Hawk. He has come to punish the black-bearded one and his iron hearts."

For a second Hawk wondered how Tames Horses

could have known he was in this high, mountain country, then he remembered the two Nez Percé girls he had saved from Bannister's men.

"I guess them two women got back to your village safely."

"They say giant white man save them. They say he has golden mane and blue eyes. They say he drop like bird from the sky, like thunderbolt. When I hear this, I know it is Golden Hawk. Now you must meet this war chief of the Yellow Grass band. He wait long time for this honor."

Tames Horses turned and beckoned to the Nez Percé chief, who was sitting his horse patiently about ten yards back. At once the chief spurred his pony toward them, and when he pulled up alongside them, Tames Horses introduced him to Hawk as Chief Sun Walker.

Sun Walker's face looked as if it had been chipped out of granite. A solid, rigid brow kept his gleaming coal-black eyes in shadow. More impressive still was the number of eagle feathers crowding his bonnet, each one testifying to a verified coup earned in battle. The chief seemed barely able to contain himself—as if he had some momentous secret to share.

Hawk raised his palm in salute. "I am honored to meet a famed war chief of the Nez Percé," Hawk told him in the Indian's language. "Especially one with so many feathers in his bonnet."

"And I am honored to meet the great Golden Hawk," Sun Walker replied with solemn dignity, "the scourge of the hated and treacherous Blackfoot."

Hawk said nothing more, just nodded. Otherwise, they would have gone on all morning trading compliments.

Nudging his pony still closer, the chief asked, "Does Golden Hawk have sister?"

Surprised at the question, Hawk replied, "Yes, Chief."

"She lives still?"

"Yes, Chief."

"This make Sun Walker glad."

"You know my sister?"

"When Sun Walker is young brave he is captured by the Blood chief Tall Buffalo of the Red Blanket band. In Red Blanket village Sun Walker see the sister of Golden Hawk. She is the woman of Tall Buffalo. The Blackfoot women cut Sun Walker many times and burn him with iron brands." He paused, savoring the memory of the torture he had endured and of his defiance in the face of it. "Sun Walker does no cry out. He is ready to die. But in the night Golden Hawk's sister cut Sun Walker free. She give him food and help him escape. Now Sun Walker is back with his people and is great chief."

Hawk smiled. "Know this, Sun Walker, my sister is no longer with Tall Buffalo. She has escaped and lives now in California. She has a white husband and enjoys good health. I am sure she thinks many times of the brave warrior she helped set free from his Blackfoot captors."

The war chief could not quench his delight. "What Golden Hawk say make this chief's heart soar like the eagle! Now Golden Hawk will be the guest of the Yellow Grass band. And he will meet again the two he saved."

Pulling his horse around, he rode proudly back to the waiting Nez Percé warriors.

Frowning, Hawk turned to Tames Horses. "Tell the chief I'm sorry, but I can't accept his invitation. Not right now, anyway. I've got to help these men get back their womenfolk from the Blackfoot. It's not going to be easy."

"For this you are in great hurry?"

"Damn right."

"You know what I think?" Tames Horses asked slyly.

"What do you think?"

"I think maybe you have plenty time."

Hawk's eyes narrowed and he leaned closer to the Nez Percé. "You old buzzard, what are you up to?"

Tames Horses' weathered face brightened. "Why you think we come here to this fort? We have news for the Quaker men. Already in our village we have the wagon train's women and children. We see what happen and our braves do not like it. This is Nez Percé land. So we take the women and children back from the Blackfoot. We also take some Blackfoot scalps. Come, now we will bring you to our village."

Hawk laughed in amazement and delight. Relief flooded him, as well as exasperation. But it was typical. Though Tames Horses and the chief could have given him this news from the beginning, no Indian would hurry an announcement as important as this, and true to form, Tames Horses had held the news back to the very last.

"Wait here," he told Tames Horses. "I'll get the men."

*   *   *

The celebration in the Nez Percé village that night and in the night that followed was one that no man, woman, or child who participated would ever forget. The joy of the men as they were reunited with their wives and children—plus the pride the Nez Percé felt at being responsible for such joy—set a tone of love and acceptance that permeated the village. Indians and white settlers mingled as freely and as intimately as brothers and sisters. For the Quakers this was nothing less than a joyous vindication of their gentle preachments of the brotherhood of man. They had forgotten, it seemed, the evil depradations of Bannister and his men and the bloodthirsty malevolence of the Blackfoot warriors who had almost managed to carry the women and children off to slavery—or worse.

The Nez Percé brought out their finest, most precious possessions to offer as gifts. Magnificent Appaloosa horses were given to those who had lost their own horseflesh. Some chiefs offered to the men prime breeding stock so as to enable the settlers to start their own Appaloosa herds when they reached the heart of the Oregon Territory. Meanwhile, hunters had been sent out to bring fresh venison, and soon over countless fires throughout the village the rich meat was roasting.

Due to the attack on their wagon train, many of the settlers' goods had been ruined or taken, but enough had remained in the wagons or been retaken from the Blackfoot to enable them to show their gratitude with many fine gifts of their own. In addition, the Quakers turned out to be fine musicians, and the night was soon alive with the happy screech of the fiddle, the mouth harp, and the har-

monica. To this was added the drums of the Nez
Percé, and before long the settlers were teaching
the Nez Percé how to square dance, and it was soon
evident that—for this Nez Percé band, at least—a
new and delightful dance had been added to any
celebrations they might have in the future.

And throughout it all, not a single drop of whiskey flowed.

In Tames Horses' lodge, Hawk pulled off his boots
and slipped out of his pants, then lay back wearily
on his couch. Even though it was close to midnight,
the screech of the fiddle still rang in the night and
the steady boom of the drums continued to sound.
At least, Hawk told himself as he pulled off his
buckskin shirt, he did not have to listen to the
noise of drunken Indians puking up their insides to
make room for more whiskey.

He reclined on his couch, wondering idly when
Tames Horses would be back. The last he had seen
of the old warrior, he was doing his best to square-
dance with a huge Quaker woman. As Hawk pulled
the blanket over his shoulder and turned away from
the hearth, he heard Tames Horses flip aside the
entrance flap and step inside the lodge. He was
about to twist his head to greet him when a warm,
lithe body slipped under the blanket with him.

This was not Tames Horses.

Turning his head, Hawk found himself looking
into the eyes of one of the two girls he had saved
from Bannister's men. She was called Willow in
the Wind. He had been introduced to her and her
companion earlier that evening. Both had been
delighted at his fluent command of their language

and each had promised to visit him before he left. Willow in the Wind was keeping her promise.

She smiled, her bright white teeth gleaming in the darkness.

"Hello, Willow," he said.

"Shh," she said. "We must be quiet or the white women will hear us."

He slid back on the couch to make room for her. Moving with him, she stayed close, flattening her warm body against his, her hot hand reaching down to close about his growing erection. With a soft, eager grunt, she snuggled still closer. He turned to face her more directly. She thrust her warm, silken muff against his erection, lifting one leg to make it easy for him. He rammed it home.

"Ah! This is good," she murmured. "I wait long time to see the Golden Hawk again. Too long!"

"Shut up," Hawk told her. "I've waited too, Willow."

Grunting in savage eagerness, she grabbed his shoulders and pulled him over onto her, thrusting eagerly up at him as she did so. Hawk was used to a bit more foreplay, but Willow appeared to be in a very great hurry. Besides, there was really no need for him to heat up the oven. She was already lubricated nicely, and was writhing under him like a wildcat, her fingers raking down his back, plowing deep ridges.

Ignoring the damage she was doing to his back, he humped away happily, losing all track of time. In a few wild moments, she began exploding beneath him, gasping up at him and laughing with each violent spasm. She sure as hell had a short fuse, he realized.

But he was not finished yet.

At once she realized his dilemma.

"It is all right," she told him eagerly. "Now I ride you."

Pushing him back, she forked a thigh over him, then plunged recklessly down upon him, riding him with a furious, ecstatic abandon. Hawk tightened his buttocks and drove up to meet each thrust. Her long raven hair exploded out behind her as she shook her head wildly back and forth, her teeth clenched, a mewling groan coming from deep within her. Any sense of deliberation vanished as Hawk found his loins on fire. He began bucking wildly under her, completely caught up in her frenzy, thundering toward his orgasm with nothing to hold him back now, and in a few moments he had carried them both over the top.

He let the delicious relief of it wash over him and, leaning back, stretched luxuriously. But Willow remained still astride him and he was still inside her—though a much smaller part than before. His ashes had been hauled nicely.

Laughing softly, she collapsed forward onto his chest and rested her cheek on his thick mat of coiled hair. He stroked her long hair idly as his breathing slowed down. Abruptly, she lifted her head to look into his eyes, then began kissing his lips with a wild, savage intensity. Before long, to his surprise, he began answering her kiss with the same crazy abandon, and soon he was once again erect inside her. Laughing delightedly at her accomplishment, she squirmed lasciviously back down onto him, sucking him deep up into her, and then began pulsing repeatedly as she experienced a series of rapid, seemingly involuntary orgasms.

"Ummm," she murmured when at last she grew quiet. Spreading her legs slightly, she pulled back and lifted off him.

"You sure you had enough?" he asked her. He had meant it to sound sarcastic, but he could see she did not hear it that way.

"Oh, yes, I think so. But I could not stop," she told him. "Golden Hawk make me so alive again."

He chuckled softly, unwilling to see her go. She had taken his measure, but he was ready now to take hers.

"Come here," he said. "You're not going anywhere."

But she pushed him gently back. "No. I must go now. There is Soaring Bird yet. She waits outside."

Pushing herself upright, she reached for her buckskin dress and left the lodge as swiftly and as silently as she had entered. A second later, before Hawk could figure a place to hide, Soaring Bird entered.

In an effort to convince her that one woman was enough for a single human being in one night, even for the mighty Golden Hawk, he sat up and tried to get to his feet. But her dress was already over her head. An instant later it was on the floor of the lodge and she stood naked before him. She was taller than Willow, her hips wider, her midnight hair longer. And there was a fullness in her breasts that caused his heart to pound. He gave up any idea of protest. He was ready for her, come what may.

No words were needed. She stepped regally toward him, thrusting her gleaming dark triangle inches from his face. He could smell her. It was intoxicating. Then she stepped still closer and dropped onto his lap, forking him as she would a pony, her legs scissoring his waist, her pubis pressing urgently against his erection. With her arms about his neck, she arched her spine, engulfing his erection hungrily. Hawk rolled her over onto her back and planted himself deeper into her. She was snug, he found, and warm, incredibly so. He began to plunge down into her, slowly, rhythmically, unwilling to let go completely. He wanted to savor this one.

Her hot, musky Indian smell assailed his nostrils. He felt the length of her body fitted snugly against his, the incandescent warmth of her breasts pressing close against him. Looking down into her eyes was like peering into unfathomable depths—into another more savage time.

As he continued to rock with slowly building intensity, she tightened her arms about his neck, pulling his lips down hard onto hers. They were alive, probing, teasing, wanting. Tiny cries, like those emitted by small animals, broke from deep in her throat, and he honestly wondered if he were hurting her, but it didn't matter as he continued to thrust and answer her kisses.

Suddenly, she reached a hand down, caught one of his buttocks, and pulled him urgently, hungrily closer. Her meaning was clear. He began to accelerate his thrusts, increasing their depth with each plunge. But she was depthless, bottomless. He might as well have been plumbing the depths of the ocean itself. Her fiery fingers traced frantically up and down his back, adding her tracks to those left by Willow. Her tongue darted deep into his mouth, back and forth, exhibiting a wanton abandon, an ancient wizardry, the skill of ages, as their lips fought frantically in a wild, searing kiss that became a kind of wounding savagery. What they were experiencing, he realized dimly, had nothing to do with love or hate. Only brutal, searing need.

His groin churned into flame. He found himself pounding down into her, carrying himself over the edge, exploding like a string of Chinese firecrackers. She clung to him, her lips still fastened to his, her answering climax coming then too as she pulsed wildly, her arms about his neck tightening with such intensity he was afraid he was not going to be able to break free in time to regain his breath. And then her arms dropped away and she sighed, panting.

He started to withdraw.

At once she cried out angrily and raked his back again with her fingernails. What he had felt of her orgasm, he realized then, was only a preamble. He had ignited her fuse. Now came the detonations. She clung to him fiercely, and the hot, flowing warmth of her tightened convulsively about what remained of his erection. She shuddered, grew rigid, flung her head back, and let go a tiny cry, tossing frantically beneath him. It seemed to go on forever, and the hot, searing warmth enveloping his vitals renewed his erection. The smell of her intensified. Her panting increased and her hot breath seared his face. She was all savage now, lust unleashed from any reins, wild, insatiable.

Aroused now beyond anything he had experienced before, Hawk took charge. He plunged deep within her, impaling her on the couch with brutal abandon. The sudden force of his renewed thrusting caused her to gasp. Then her eyes lit, her teeth parting in a smile that was also a grimace. He drove into her again and again, holding nothing back, determined to nail her to his couch. He was part of her now, welded to her flesh, pleased at the sight of her tossing head, her wide eyes, the savage, guttural grunts that continued to break from deep within her.

She began to beat upon his chest . . . until suddenly she climaxed again. But Hawk paid no attention as he continued to pound away. He was hitting bottom this time with each stroke. Soon she was caught up once again in his violent rutting, her heels locked securely around his back, growling like an animal worrying a bone. Deeper he thrust, and still deeper . . . and suddenly she was muttering to him, calling him every evil name in the Nez Percé tongue. He laughed and kept pounding, his climax building steadily until at last he came again—a long, shuddering release that caught her up as well.

And then it was over. He rolled limply off her, his body covered with perspiration. She too was shiny with it. And the smell of their lovemaking filled the lodge. She looked deep into his eyes.

"Willow in the Wind thinks she will have Golden Hawk's child. Maybe so. But I think Soaring Bird has taken a man-child from your loins this night. I could feel him rushing into me."

"You sure of that?"

"Yes."

"What was it, anyway? A contest?"

"We both want son from you—a warrior that will make the Yellow Grass band of the Nez Percé the most famous in all these mountains. He will have your yellow hair . . . and your strength."

"I see. You and Willow visited me this night for the good of your band?"

She laughed, her white teeth gleaming in savage triumph. "Maybe that is what Willow think. But maybe I come to you because I want to feel you inside me. I want to feel your lips. I know this when first I see you punish those filthy white men and set us free."

He smiled. "I am tired, Soaring Bird. It has been a hard day, and now it has been a long night."

She sighed and shook her head in mock pity. "The great Golden Hawk. He is only a man, after all."

She leaned forward and kissed him, this time with a strange tenderness, then snatched up her dress and stepped out into the night. As he lay back on the couch, he realized for the first time that the fiddler had stopped playing. The drummer, too.

He pulled the blanket up over his shoulder and slept, like a stone falling into a black, fathomless well.

Three days later, having consented to serve as their guide, Hawk set out for the Willamette Valley at the head of the Quaker wagon train. Beside him rode Tames Horses. The old warrior had insisted on accompanying Hawk. Just once before he died, he told Hawk, he wanted to gaze upon that great expanse of water they called the Pacific.

Less than a week after leaving the Nez Percé village, approaching the Blue Mountains, Hawk and Tames Horses forded a stream late in the day in search of a campsite. When they returned, they found the stream considerably swifter than it had been when they forded it earlier—and rising rapidly. Neither Hawk nor Tames Horses was surprised. They had noticed the black clouds sitting on the western horizon.

As he and Tames Horses fought their way back across the stream, Hawk saw Caleb Tribe and Tim Holcolm standing on the bank, arguing vociferously. Gaining the eastern bank, Hawk and Tames Horses rode over to them.

"What's all this, Caleb?" Hawk said, dismounting. "You won't get the wagons across the stream this way."

Tribe, who had been elected the wagon train's captain, addressed Hawk with some heat. "Tim says we ought to wait until tomorrow before crossing. He says we should camp on this side of the stream."

Holcolm jumped in then. "Hawk, it's the women. They don't want to make camp with their bedding and everything wet. It'll be impossible for them to cook supper. Why not wait and get an early start in the morning?"

"Because you won't get an early start in the morning," Hawk replied. "There's storms in the mountains ahead. A lot of rain's coming, and this is the season for it. If you wait much longer, this stream will be too high to cross—and it'll be a week before it subsides, if it does then. Cross now or camp on this side for a week."

"See that?" Tribe said, turning to Holcolm.

"But look at that stream now, Hawk," Tim said, ignoring Tribe. "How we goin' to cross it? You two made it on your horses, but we've got wagons to bring across."

Hawk glanced at Tribe. "You mind if Tames Horses and I give you hand?"

"I'd sure appreciate it, Hawk."

"Water the horses thoroughly. We don't want them bogging down in the middle of the stream to take a drink. Then line up the wagons, and wait."

Hawk mounted up, and after a short discussion, he and Tames Horses rode off to gather willow sticks, then rode back out into the stream to locate the shifting sandbars and gravel beds closest to the surface. Wherever they found the streambed sufficiently solid for a ford, they planted their sticks on both sides of it until they had marked it out clear to the other side. The strong current had shifted the sand and gravel, so that the ford now slanted diagonally downstream before it reached the far shore. But with the willow sticks as a guide, the wagons could stay on the ford and make it safely across.

If they wasted no time . . .

Hawk and Tames Horses waved Tribe and four or five of the men over to the far side. They mounted up on saddle horses and splashed across. Under Hawk's direction, they worked swiftly to shore up the bank with brush and fresh earth to make it easier for the horse teams when they gained the far bank.

Splashing back across the stream, Hawk rode over to Tim Holcolm, who was up on the seat of the first wagon, the reins wrapped about his left fist, the whip in his right hand. His wife was crouched behind him in the wagon, peeking out fearfully at the steadily rising water.

"Once you start across," Hawk told Holcolm, "keep going, or the wheels will start sinking in. Don't stop for anything."

Holcolm nodded grimly, cracked his whip, and let out a war whoop. The team plunged into the water, and keeping between the willow sticks, Holcolm made the far shore with hardly a pause, even though the water at times surged almost as high as the wagon bed. His example was a good one, and six more wagons piled rapidly into the stream after him, gaining the far shore safely.

With the seventh and the last wagon trouble developed. This wagon belonged to the patriarch of the party, Elias Smithers. His wife, Sarah, sat perched on the seat beside him wielding the whip, as tough and determined as her husband, stoutly unwilling to cower in the wagon as had the other women. They did well enough until they reached the middle of the stream, where Smithers' team— the four oldest horses in the group—lost any forward momentum and began floundering helplessly, allowing the wagon's wheels to sink deep into the chewed-up sand and gravel.

Hawk and Tames Horses rode out into the stream. Hawk caught the lead horse's bridle and began tugging the animal on. The old draft horse, eyes bugging out of its head, redoubled its efforts, but so mired was the wagon by this time that the team seemed unable to budge it an inch closer to the far shore. Meanwhile, Tames Horses had circled around the wagon and was sending his horsewhip exploding over the team. The snapping whip added a sense of urgency to the situation, but it had little practical effect on the horses' ability to haul the wagon any farther. In fact, the wagon's wheels appeared to be sinking still deeper, while the steadily rising current, the powerful waters battering with increasing fury at the wagon's sides, threatened at any moment to slam the wagon onto its side and send its occupants and contents swirling on down the stream.

Hawk took out his revolver and fired it close over the heads of the horses. Then he thumb-cocked and fired again.

This made the difference.

Eyes starting out of their heads, the terrified animals leapt and jumped in their traces, freeing the wagon's wheels in a single, wrenching movement. Hawk fired a third round and the team charged frantically on across the stream until their hooves gained purchase on the solid streambed nearer the shore. A moment later, with Hawk pulling the lead horse along, the horses gained the embankment and charged up it to come to a shivering, stamping halt in the midst of the waiting wagons.

As Elias Smithers looped his reins around the brake handle and helped his wife down, the rest of the settlers rushed over, cheering and throwing their hats into the air. For a moment back there, it had not looked good for them.

Dismounting, Hawk and Tames Horses walked back to the edge of the stream. Hawk had not been nearly as sure as he had sounded when he had agreed with Tribe that they should make the crossing without waiting. Now, as he stood beside Tames Horses and watched the last of the willow branches being swept under, he realized he had cut things pretty damn close. The stream was rising with astonishing speed, at a faster rate than only a few minutes before. Swirling currents battered and chewed voraciously at the shore, while the current in the center of the stream was so swift the surface looked as slick as ice. Branches and tree trunks from farther upstream began to sweep past.

Tames Horses turned to Hawk. "I think you crazy man. Why you in such a hurry to get across this wild water?"

"I want to catch someone."

"Ah," said Tames Horses. "I understand. It is that man Bannister you want."

Hawk nodded. He had no intention of letting Bannister sell Marta Baldwin into slavery, and as soon as he reached the Oregon coast, he would search out the clipper-ship captain young Sam had told him about, the one who was so anxious to sell Marta Baldwin to a Middle Eastern potentate.

Tames Horses looked back at the stream. "Golden Hawk's medicine is still powerful, I think. We do not lose a single wagon. Maybe you will get Bannister. And I will help."

"Thanks, Tames Horses. I'm counting on it."

"And now maybe I tell you something else."

"What's that?"

"For two days now I see sign. We are being followed."

"By Blackfoot?"

"You see sign, too?"

"Some. But I wasn't sure. Once, a faint trail of smoke in the morning. A mounted warrior on a ridge in the distance. Could just be a Flathead hunting party, I figured."

"No. Not Flathead. Blackfoot war party. They

not like the way the Yellow Grass band scalp their brothers, I think. Now maybe they come to take what Bannister promise them."

Hawk sighed. "This is a big-enough wagon train. We're all armed, and they know it. Maybe they'll see that and go back. They're a long way from home."

"Maybe they go back like you say. But I don't think so."

Neither did Hawk.

The two men left the stream bank and headed back to their horses. They still had to lead the wagon train to the campsite they had selected. It was a good mile farther on—a fine, brook-fed meadow, a spot from which they could see the towering peaks of the distant Blue Mountains.

And plenty of open space around the wagons, so there'd be no chance of a surprise attack.

— 4 —

The pass beckoned to them in the distance, a welcome break in the jagged rampart of snow-capped peaks shouldering into the sky. A long, narrow ridge clothed in pine ran south of the pass. Beyond it, the towering, sheer walls of the gap were clearly visible. So sudden and stark was the cleft in the mountain range, it almost seemed to have been sliced out with the measured strokes of a titanic ax.

Tames Horses had ridden ahead to scout. Hawk, astride his black, was riding alongside Tim Holcolm's lead wagon, talking quietly to Tim as they moved across the long, sweeping grassland rising steadily toward the pass.

"A mighty pretty sight, that pass," Holcolm remarked, stroking his black, neatly trimmed beard. "Means we'll be through this range before long, and a week or two more should bring us to the Willamette Valley. It's been a long, grueling trip. I can hardly believe we're this close."

"Don't count your chickens," Hawk reminded him.

"You still worried about them Blackfoot?"

"I always worry about Blackfoot."

"I figure we've left them far behind. That raging stream back there must've stopped them, surely."

"Maybe."

Hawk had no desire to trouble Holcolm or any of the others. Not unless he had to. So he let Holcolm believe what he wanted to believe. But Hawk never knew of a Blackfoot that could be stopped by anything as inconsequential as a swollen stream. And one reason why Tames Horses had ridden ahead to check out the pass was that he had been catching a lot of sign lately. The Blackfoot were so sure of themselves, they were getting careless.

And that pass would be a great place for them to spring their trap.

Holcolm began to chat with his wife in the wagon behind him. She was a cheerful woman with graying red hair, a pale, freckled complexion, and blue eyes staring in their intensity. What she wanted was for her husband to stop or slow down long enough to let her get down so she could walk back to visit Tribe's wife in the wagon behind. Tim consented to slow down, and with that his wife ducked back inside the wagon to get her bonnet.

Hawk sent his black into a lope and rode on ahead, his eyes searching for a sign of Tames Horses. As his eyes swept to the right, he saw a herd of antelope moving off in long, soaring leaps. He wasn't sure, but he thought he saw a wolf pack strung out along the horizon, keeping their collective eyes on the antelope band.

It was truly beautiful country.

He kept going and was a good half-mile ahead of the wagons when he caught sight of Tames Horses galloping through the tall grass toward him. Hawk booted his horse to a gallop and rode to meet him.

"Blackfoot," Tames Horses called out to Hawk as soon as they were close enough. "Large war party. Twenty, maybe more braves. Famous war chief Red Feather lead them. I know of him. He very tough."

"In the pass?" Hawk asked, pulling up.

Tames Horses nodded, reining in beside Hawk. "If wagons go into pass, they not come out."

Hawk glanced over at the southern ridge he had noticed earlier. "Check out that ridge over there," he said, pointing to it. "We could make a pretty good stand there. I'll go back and tell Holcolm what we're up against."

With a quick nod, the old warrior wheeled his pony and set off for the ridge. Hawk watched him go for a moment, then studied the ridge toward which he was riding. Satisfied that it represented their best chance, Hawk turned his black and headed back to the wagon train.

Riding up to Holcolm's wagon, Hawk told Holcolm to hold up. Holcolm hauled back on his reins. The wagons behind creaked to a halt also. Hawk dismounted, Holcolm climbed down from his wagon, and Caleb Tribe came running. When Hawk told them what was waiting for them in the pass ahead, Tribe's face went as white as paper.

"My God, Jed. Is Tames Horses sure they're Blackfoot?"

Hawk just looked at Tribe

"Okay," said a very nervous Holcolm. "So what do we do now, Hawk?"

"One thing's for sure: we can't take these wagons into that pass."

"But we can't go back," Tribe said.

"I know that, Caleb. Our best bet is to head for that ridge south of the pass. From there we should be able to hold off the Blackfoot until our combined firepower discourages them."

"But if they see us veer away from the pass," Holcolm pointed out, "won't they know we're onto them?"

"They sure will. But maybe we can fool them."

"How?"

"Keep on toward the pass until we're almost there. Then, at the last minute, turn our wagons and make for the ridge."

"The moment we do that," Holcolm pointed out, "they'll be out of that pass after us."

Hawk nodded. "Which means we better reach that ridge before they do."

"Ain't that cutting it close?" Tribe asked.

"Very close. And we don't have much time. Get on your horse, Tribe. Ride back and tell the others."

Untying his saddle horse from the rear of his wagon, Tribe mounted up and started back along the wagon train, spreading the word.

Hawk could understand how this unwelcome news would affect the settlers, and as they stepped down from their wagons to talk it over, Hawk saw on their faces first disbelief, then dismay. Then anger. They had come so far, had endured so much. Was there to be no end to their trials?

Before long Hawk saw, blazing in their eyes, a stubborn, resolute determination to go on—come what may.

Tribe rode back. "Okay, Hawk. Lead the way."

Hawk checked his rifle's load and mounted up.

Holcolm got back up onto his wagon's seat and picked up the reins, and the rest of the settlers returned to their wagons. With a single wave to Holcolm, Hawk moved out in front of the wagon train and headed straight for the distant pass. The plan was simple enough. When Hawk judged they were close enough to the pass, he was to take off his hat and wave it.

Then all hell would break loose.

With the sheer white cliffs of the pass filling the sky in front of him, Hawk decided they had gone far enough. Lifting his hat, he waved it once, then swung his horse and at full gallop led the wagons south to the ridge. Behind Hawk came the sound of cracking whips and shrill whistles. Glancing back over his shoulder, he saw the horses straining in their traces and the men standing up on their seats as they urged their horses to greater speed.

He turned back around to see Tames Horses galloping toward him. He was pointing at the pass. Hawk looked over and saw the Blackfoot band boiling out of the cleft. Tames Horses' estimate of the war party's size had been modest. There had to be more than twenty braves in this war party.

As soon as Tames Horses reached Hawk, he swung around and led Hawk and the wagons toward the ridge and up a narrow, chutelike gully that went to its top. Once the wagons had been drawn into a circle, Hawk left Holcolm and four others behind to guard them; then he and Tames Horses took the rest of the men down the face of the ridge to meet the Blackfoot charge.

Hawk spread six men out to the right of the

gully, while Caleb Tribe moved to the left of it and dug in with five men spaced between him and Hawk. On the ridge behind them, Holcolm seemed to be taking charge nicely. Hawk was satisfied for the moment.

Meanwhile, the Blackfoot band, instead of charging directly at the dug-in defenders, had pulled up and dismounted some distance from the ridge and were standing in a great circle. There was much waving of hands and shaking of heads. What they were doing, Hawk realized, was building themselves up to the chore that lay ahead. At last, fortified, they finished their palaver, broke apart, and leapt astride their ponies.

"Here they come," Tribe called. "See to your priming, men."

Beside Hawk, Tames Horses moved up the slope a ways and ducked behind a boulder, his rifle at the ready. Hawk watched as the mounted Blackfoot loped toward them in a long, ragged line. Occasionally a brave broke from the line and charged ahead of the others, waving his lance and hurling insults before wheeling and darting back to his comrades.

"There," said Tames Horses, pointing. "Red Feather!"

Hawk had no difficulty picking out the Blackfoot war chief with the single red feather stuck in his headband. Lifting his rifle, he rested his sight on the Blackfoot, waiting for him to get closer. Abruptly, Red Feather flung up his hand, halting the Blackfoot charge. Dismounting, the Blackfoot continued their advance on foot, slipping through the tall grass. Hawk cursed. The grass provided damn good cover, and before long the Blackfoot were soon out of sight. Only an occasional movement of the grass betrayed their presence as they sneaked through the rippling grassland, like fish swimming beneath its surface.

Hawk heard one of the Quaker's curse. It was not what Hawk had come to expect from such men, but Hawk could understand perfectly the man's frustration.

"Dammit," another man muttered loudly. "I can't see a single one of 'em."

"Don't worry," his neighbor told him. "You will soon enough."

A fourth man, equally frustrated, stood up and craned his head to get a better view. A shot from a clump of grass sent a slug ricocheting off a rock inches from his head. He ducked so quickly, it looked as if he had been shot.

"Maybe you can't see em, Deke," Tribe drawled. "But they sure as hell can see you."

The man called Deke shrank still lower, his face chalk-white.

Without warning, rifle fire erupted from the grass, the slugs whining like angry hornets about the men crouched in the rocks. Then, uttering shrill war cries, the Blackfoot leapt upright and charged the ridge's defenders.

As coolly as possible, Hawk and the others opened up on the charging Blackfoot. Two warriors spun to the ground. Another was wounded enough to go down on one knee. The other Blackfoot darted back into the grass.

"We've licked them," a settler cried.

The rest of the men started a cheer.

"Hold it down," Hawk cried. "It ain't over yet. They'll be back. Keep your positions."

Tames Horses joined Hawk. "Soon it will be dusk. They will come then, I think."

All around him, Hawk could hear the men moving about the boulders, doing their best to shore up their defenses. It was a good idea.

"I'm going back up to the ridge to check on the wagons," Hawk told Tames Horses.

Tames Horses nodded. Hawk hurried back up the slope to the crest of the ridge. Holcolm had deployed his men well. They were dug in just inside the ring of wagons. If the Blackfoot made it this far, they would be faced with a murderous fusillade from under the wagons. He found also that Holcolm had set the women to loading spare rifles and revolvers, in the event that the issue were to be decided up there among the wagons.

Hawk returned to Tames Horses. As the old Nez Percé had predicted, the next attack came just as dusk was falling and was led by a foolish brave more anxious for renown than a long life. Rising from the grass and firing as he came, the warrior dashed toward the dug-in settlers, brandishing only a knife. He got as far as the rocks just below before someone planted a hole in his chest. Yet somehow he kept coming, a ragged line of Blackfoot warriors following him up the slope bordering the gulley.

The wounded Blackfoot turned in Hawk's direction. Hawk aimed carefully and sent a round at him. The Indian spun, then, miraculously, came on again. As swiftly as he could, Hawk reloaded his rifle. The brave was less than ten yards from him when Hawk swung up his barrel and fired. This round nicked the Blackfoot's side just under his rib cage. As good as a miss. Hawk was reaching for his

Colt when the Indian slammed into him, the force of his charge knocking Hawk back against the slope.

The Indian still had his knife. As he raised it over his head to plunge it into Hawk's chest, Hawk reached up with both hands and grabbed his wrist. Gathering his feet under him, he lunged upward. Hawk had better than fifty pounds on the Blackfoot, most of it muscle. He twisted the Blackfoot's wrist. It snapped like a dry twig.

Hawk kicked the Indian back down the slope as another Blackfoot came at him from his right. Hawk swung his Colt around and fired, catching this one in the belly. The Blackfoot fell facedown onto the rocky slope. Glancing to his left, Hawk saw Tames Horses swing his rifle like a club, bringing it down on the head of a charging Blackfoot. The warrior spun about, then staggered blindly back down the slope, both hands clasped about his bloody head. From both sides of the gulley came the crackle of rifle and pistol fire, along with the sound of desperate men locked in hand-to-hand combat. Then, almost as quickly as it had begun, the attack ended and the Indians turned and vanished back into the grass.

Tames Horses looked over at Hawk. "They be back," he said, "when night comes."

Hawk set off along the slope to see how much damage the Blackfoot had inflicted on the defenders. In all, he found only two men with minor flesh wounds, both inflicted with knives, and one man with a bloody gash on the side of his head, the result of a deflected war hatchet. He had bled like a stuck pig, but the wound looked worse than it was.

Let the night come, Hawk thought as he moved back up the slope. It was completely dark when he reached the top of the ridge and started for the wagons. He was within a few feet of Holcolm's wagon when a dark figure strode into his path, his rifle at the ready.

"That you, Hawk?" It was Holcolm.

"It's me, all right."

"Better whistle next time," Holcolm said, lowering his rifle. "I almost squeezed this trigger."

"I guess I should have called out."

"We heard the shooting. Anyone hurt bad?"

Hawk gave Holcolm a full report as they entered the ring of wagons. No campfires had been lit for obvious reasons, and when Hawk saw the pale faces of the women peering at him out of the darkness, he felt a pang of concern. Though they remained in control, it was obvious the sound of gunfire from below had left them terrified.

"They'll be back tonight," Hawk told Holcolm. "And I think you can expect some of them to try to make it up that draw. You think you can hold it if they do?"

"We'll have to."

"They're a real tenacious bunch, Tim," Hawk said. "It takes a lot to bring them down."

"It'll be just as hard for them to bring us down."

"Keep the women and children inside the wagons. They can hand down those loaded rifles from there."

Holcolm nodded.

Hawk reached the side of the draw and squinted into the black maw yawning up at him. Out of that devil's hole would surge the toughest Blackfoot,

Hawk realized, warriors even more determined than those they had met below. And once loose among the wagons, they would raise havoc. If Holcolm and his men failed to cut them down, the Blackfoot would have Hawk and those men with him under fire from above and below.

A bloody massacre would follow.

When Hawk left Holcolm to return to Tames Horses and the others, he said only, "We're relying on you, Tim."

"Don't worry," the man said, stroking his beard, his dark eyes gleaming in the night. "We've come this far. We're not going to be stopped now."

And Hawk believed him.

It was quiet. Ominously quiet. There had been no move from Red Feather since the attack at dusk. The moon—a bright, harvest moon—hung like a streetlamp over the grassland below. Hawk checked his rifle one more time, then loosened the Colt in his belt. It was only a matter of time, he knew.

Two braves led the assault on Hawk's position. Hawk stopped one with his rifle, then resorted to his Colt, catching the second one high in the chest, spinning him back into the darkness. As Hawk reloaded his rifle, he saw Tames Horses pick off a charging Blackfoot warrior as calmly as a farmer at a turkey shoot.

Steady rifle fire echoed up and down the slope. Cries filled the night. A Blackfoot brave started up the slope toward Hawk. He fired. The Blackfoot stopped, then vanished behind a pile of rocks. Hawk heard the sole of a moccasin scrape the surface of a rock behind him. Swinging his Colt around, he fired up at the figure hurtling at him out of the night. The sweaty body struck him with a numbing blow. Hawk dropped his Colt. But the Indian was lifeless. Hawk straightened and flung the dead body off him.

The Blackfoot he had wounded a moment before reappeared then, driving up the slope toward him. There was no time for Hawk to find his Colt in the darkness. He unsheathed his bowie and, raising his left forearm, warded off his attacker's war hatchet; with his right he drove the blade of his bowie deep into the Blackfoot's chest. The brave gasped. Hawk withdrew the knife, felt the sudden gush of warm blood that followed after it, then he pushed the Blackfoot back down the slope.

He heard a scuffle to his left. Swinging about, he saw Tames Horses ramming the barrel of his rifle deep into the midsection of an attacking Blackfoot. Behind the old warrior another Blackfoot was materializing out of the night. Reaching back, Hawk sent his throwing knife through the air, the spinning blade sinking into the warrior's throat. Gagging, his chest gleaming with the sudden wash of blood, the Blackfoot sank to the ground. Tames Horses retrieved Hawk's throwing knife and tossed it back to him.

"Back up to the wagons," Hawk cried, snatching up his Colt and grabbing his rifle.

As Hawk and the others took cover behind the wagons, Holcolm and his defenders opened up on the Blackfoot rushing up the ridge after them. For almost an hour longer the battle raged. Only a few of Red Feather's braves managed to break through the wagons, and they were promptly disposed of with side arms at close range.

When the frontal assault proved fruitless, Red Feather attempted to burn them out. But Hawk had alerted the women. Buckets of water were ready beside each wagon. The first burning arrow was ripped from the wagon's canvas and tossed to the ground by Holcolm's angry wife. Other wagons were set afire as well, but the buckets of water were put to good use and the flames guttered out.

The flaming arrows were no longer plunging out of the night.

All was quiet. Too quiet. Suddenly, near dawn, Smithers' wife, Sarah, let out a heart-stopping screech from inside her wagon. Hawk raced over and peered in, to see Elias grappling with a Blackfoot. Hawk leapt in, grabbed the savage by one of his braids, and flung him out of the wagon. As soon as he hit the ground, the Blackfoot was set upon by the rest of the women. They used broom handles, shovels, even hammers. Under their furious ministrations, the hapless Indian did not last long.

The attack petered out. The night grew silent. And then the only sound was that of a few women in their wagons crying softly—from a delayed reaction of sheer terror or out of a feeling of relief, Hawk could not be sure.

Just before dawn, Hawk and Tames Horses returned to the rocks at the base of the ridge to study the situation. The Blackfoot war party had lit a campfire. The dim shadows of their ponies were visibly cropping the grass around them. The Blackfoot did not appear to be going anywhere soon, and this was a real disappointment to Hawk. Three of his men had been wounded this night, one of whom might lose a leg.

Meanwhile, time was passing. Valuable time. With each day that went by, Bannister would be closer to the coast and that damned clipper captain. Hawk turned to Tames Horses and handed him the Hawken.

"Hold this for me."

"Where you go now?"

"The only way to stop this is to stop Red Feather."

"How you do that?"

"That grass can hide a white man as easy as it can a Blackfoot."

Tames Horses, wrinkled face showed concern, but he said nothing as he took the rifle from Hawk.

"What are you two up to?" asked Tribe, hurrying down the slope toward them.

"No time to explain, Caleb," Hawk told him. "Just keep an eye out. I might be coming back here in a big hurry. Get some men to help cover me when I do."

Tribe wanted to hear more, but Hawk wouldn't sit still for explanations. This would only work if he could get there while it was still dark. He slipped quickly down the slope and into the high grass. When he was within a hundred or so yards of the Blackfoot campfire, he went down on all fours and crawled until he was close enough to smell the Blackfoot ponies. From that point on, he advanced on his belly, using only his knees and elbows for locomotion, slipping through the grass like a large snake. Soon he heard a pony stamping the ground beside him to his right. He paused long enough to catch the hum of Blackfoot voices. He headed directly for them, until he caught the glow of their campfire through the tall grass.

An urgent Blackfoot parley was in progress. Hawk could hear the debate with reasonable clarity. One voice dominated. That of Red Feather, Hawk had no doubt. It was low, powerful—at times threatening. Fluent in Blackfoot, Hawk followed the argument closely. Some braves were anxious to return to their lands before the first snows fell. Others maintained that under Red Feather's leadership, the war party's losses had been too costly. More than a few pointed out that Golden Hawk was himself guiding this wagon train—reason enough to break off the attack.

To all these arguments, Red Feather's powerful voice responded with sharp contempt, lacerating those fainthearts who wanted to pull back before the first snows, and mocking the courage of those braves unwilling to continue the attack, reminding them of the shame and ridicule they would all suffer if they returned to their village empty-handed, with not a single scalp and no booty at all to show for their losses and their long weeks of pursuit.

He finished up by reminding them that there was no source of water on the ridge, that all they had to do was lay siege to the settlers and wait for thirst to weaken their resolve, then attack. Then they would reap a harvest of scalps—including that of Golden Hawk. With the settlers' wagons filled with booty and the women and children in tow, they would return to their village in triumph, and all of them would share in the glory.

Every member of the war party got his chance to counter Red Feather's arguments, but when they finished, remembering Red Feather's scorn and his certainty that success would follow a short siege of the settlers' wagons, the war party agreed to remain and continue the assault. Hawk sighed. Despite their losses, the war party would not be pulling out. Instead, they would establish a more or less permanent camp on this meadow. And from the discussion following their decision to remain, Hawk learned they were planning to search out fresh game in the surrounding hills, leaving only a small contingent behind to harass the settlers.

Hawk glanced up at the sky. It was still dark overhead, but the eastern horizon was rapidly growing lighter. The dawn's first light would soon flood the grassland with the suddenness of a door opening into a dark room. Hawk would have to move quickly—or not at all.

The warriors sitting about the fire stood up, the flames highlighting their faces as they started for their ponies. Hawk caught sight of Red Feather, his flat face impassive and cold with resolve as he headed for his pony.

Hawk's luck was holding.

The pony toward which Red Feather was making was less than ten feet from where Hawk crouched. Hawk could hear the other Blackfoot moving away from him toward their own ponies. Red Feather loomed nearer to Hawk, then passed so close that Hawk could have reached out and tackled him. Instead, he withdrew his bowie from its sheath and pressed himself flat in the grass as Red Feather reached his pony. Red Feather took a moment to adjust his saddle board in preparation for mounting. Leaping to his feet, Hawk raced like a thunderbolt through the grass toward Red Feather.

Behind him, Hawk could hear the Blackfoot warriors shouting a warning. Red Feather swung about. Without hesitating, Hawk drove into Red Feather, slamming his left forearm against his windpipe, sending the warrior back hard against his pony. His windpipe shattered, the Indian gasped, his eyes bugging out. Before Red Feather could reach up, Hawk buried his knife hilt-deep into the savage's heart.

Snatching up the reins to Red Feather's pony, Hawk vaulted onto its back and kicked it into a fast gallop toward the ridge. A thunder of hooves exploded behind him as the Blackfoot tried desperately to overtake him. The air was filled with their war cries. Arrows and lances snicked past Hawk. Drawing his Colt, Hawk flung shots over his shoulder at those pursuers closest to him. One pony went down, throwing its rider, and behind it a warrior flung up his arms and slid off his pony.

Hawk leaned low over the pony's neck, urging it on to greater speed. He was close to the ridge now and saw Tames Horses scrambling behind a boulder on the edge of the meadow. He began to fire on the pursuing Indians. Those men on the slope above him opened up on the Blackfoot as well. The fusillade took its toll and the Blackfoot warriors peeled off and galloped back to their encampment.

Reaching the slope, Hawk flung himself from Red Feather's pony and twisted about to watch the fleeing Blackfoot. Recalling the parley he had just overheard, he knew that the remaining Blackfoot had to be more than simply dispirited about their raid.

As Tribe and the other men poured down the slope toward him, Hawk approached Tames Horses.

The Indian stepped out from behind the boulder and handed Hawk's rifle back to him. Tames Horses had made excellent use of it. The barrel was still hot.

"Thanks, Tames Horses."

"Red Feather dead?"

Hawk nodded. "Unless he can live with a crushed windpipe and a knife in his heart."

A ragged cheer erupted from the men. Hawk looked up and saw Caleb Tribe on his feet, pointing.

"There they go," he cried.

At that moment the sun's glowing eye broke over the horizon, streaking the sky with blood, its pure morning light surging across the meadow. Squinting into this molten glow, Hawk saw the Blackfoot war party riding slowly away from their encampment, their dead slung over the backs of their ponies, their wounded sagging forward as they rode. They were heading into the rising sun on their way back to their winter quarters on the northern plains.

Hawk had read their mood correctly. With their war chief dead, the Blackfoot war party had lost all heart for further battle.

An hour later, as the wagons were getting ready to move out, Tames Horses pulled his pony alongside Hawk.

"Where is your bowie?" the Indian asked Hawk.

Hawk shrugged. "Last I knew, Red Feather was wearing it in his chest. I didn't have time to pull it out."

Tames Horses reached into his parfleche and produced a knife with a white bone handle attached with rawhide. He handed it to Hawk. Hawk took the knife and hefted it. It had fine balance, and the handle fitted nicely into his palm. As sharp as a razor, the blade was at least six inches long.

"When I make this knife, I think of you," Tames Horses said. "The grip is made for Golden Hawk's hand."

"It is a fine knife," Hawk replied. "I like its balance."

Tames Horses handed to Hawk the knife's buckskin sheath. "It is yours," he said.

Hawk slipped the long blade into the buckskin sheath. Discarding his old sheath, Hawk slipped the loop of the new one through his belt, then buckled it snugly. Hawk patted the knife. It felt light and was quite comfortable, he noticed.

"I will find much use for the knife, Tames Horses," Hawk told the old Nez Percé. "It is a fine gift. This child thanks you."

The Indian's seamed face lightened in a warm smile, his dark eyes gleaming.

"It is a knife fit for Golden Hawk," he said solemnly.

Tames Horses wheeled his pony and rode into the gulley, Hawk following him closely. Behind them the wagons lurched forward, the sound of their rattle and the uneven chorus of snapping whips filling the late-morning stillness.

Hawk felt enormous relief. They were on their way again.

— 5 —

Two days beyond the pass, the day dawned damp and chill. As the wagons set out, Hawk noticed the glowering bank of black clouds rolling toward them from the west. Before long they had completely obscured the sun, and a cold, steady drizzle descended. As the trail continued to lift steeply under the wagons, the rain gradually turned to snow, which began to accumulate with startling speed.

Soon the entire wagon train was moving through a snow squall so fierce that at times Hawk had difficulty seeing more than two wagons in a row behind him, the rest having been swallowed up completely. Tames Horses rode uncomplaining beside Hawk, but Hawk saw the warrior wincing as his hunched body tensed against the frigid blast.

"Hawk!" Holcolm called from his wagon. "Keep in sight. It's you I'll be following."

Hawk raised his arm in acknowledgment, then turned to Tames Horses. "Why don't you ride in Holcolm's wagon?"

"I am not old woman," Tames Horses grumbled. And Hawk was sorry he had made the suggestion.

As they rode on through the storm, there were

occasional breaks in the shifting squalls, enabling
Hawk to catch glimpses of the high, treeless parkland
over which they crawled. They were already above
the timberline and still climbing. The snow grew
deeper, the wind more cruel. Following Tames
Horses' example, Hawk drew a blanket from his
bedroll and threw it over his shoulders. He was
forced to squint almost continuously as the sleetlike
snow lashed at his face, stinging his cheeks raw
and digging at his eyelids. It felt like he was being
pelted with needles.

On through the long, miserable day they traveled. Hawk became aware of an ominous darkness
as a great, shouldering wing of a mountain leaned
high above them, shutting out the sky. Peering to
his right through the driving snow, Hawk glimpsed
the mountain wall that now hemmed them in. Riding to the left, Tames Horses vanished for a short
while into the white maelstrom, then rode back out
of it toward Hawk.

"Over there is big drop," he shouted through the
howling wind. "Better we stay near wall."

Hawk nodded grimly. He knew of this exposed
ridge, having traveled this route before, and was
aware it was no place for them to stop. Once they
did, this first snow of the season would pile onto
this ridge, burying them. For the rest of the fall
and on through winter, the snowfall at this altitude
was almost constant, attaining a depth close to thirty
or more feet before the spring thaws commenced.

They had no choice but to keep going.

About half an hour later, as night finally closed
over them, Holcolm cried out, "Hawk! We better
hold up, make camp!"

Hawk twisted in his saddle. The snow-covered settler was holding reins that were now white with iced snow. He looked like an unhappy St. Nicholas.

"No," Hawk shouted back at him. "Keep going! If we get caught on this ridge, we'll never make it. They won't find our bones till spring."

"How can we go on through this?" Holcolm demanded as he stood up on his seat and looked behind him. "Our horses are near done, and I can't see any of the other wagons. We've left them behind."

"Keep going, damn it! If we pull up now, we'll be buried before morning. Those wagons that can't follow we'll just have to abandon."

Somewhat chastened, Holcolm slumped back down on his wagon seat and flipped his ice-encrusted reins against the backs of his weary horses. As the wagon started up again behind Tames Horses, Hawk dropped back and waited for the other wagons to show. When they appeared, he saw they were keeping in line, moving on doggedly through the snow, each wagon following the tracks of the wagon in front.

He rode back to rejoin Tames Horses.

The night became a screeching, infernal darkness, but Hawk and Tames Horses kept going, staying less than ten yards in front of Holcolm's wagon, their horses helping to break a path through the drifts for Tim's team. The swirling snow tore at Hawk's face and eyes. His cheekbones and nose stung now with a touch of frostbite, and his hands, protected clumsily with torn strips of blanket, were almost numb.

And then they were beyond the ridge, the heavy

shoulder of the mountain slipped behind them. As they continued across the treeless parkland, the snow flew straight at Hawk, even as the land kept lifting under him. But Hawk was comforted by this, since it meant they were on course, still heading due west.

Hawk glanced back repeatedly. Through breaks in the wind-whipped clouds of snow, he caught momentary glimpses of the wagons following them. As long as they kept up and managed to stay in one another's tracks, they would make it. But if any of them lagged too far behind, allowing the wind to obliterate the tracks of the wagon before them, they would wander off, eventually bogging down in a howling universe of snow and wind—to be heard from no more.

The ground beneath Hawk's black at last began to level off. Hawk felt it at once. He looked over at Tames Horses and saw that the old warrior had noticed it as well. Before long, the trail began to drop slightly, and Hawk's black was laboring less. They reached the timberline. Almost at once, it seemed, the snow slackened off. Though for at least another hour the wind-driven snow whipped at them, its fury was rapidly losing its sting.

Tall timber closed about the trail. The snow became a cold, drenching rain. Visibility markedly improved as they went on down the trail that wound now through timbered slopes. The rain petered out. The sky above them lightened. Sunlight slanted through the enormous pines. When Hawk caught sight of a level benchland just off the trail ahead, he pulled up and, turning to look back at Holcolm, gestured at it.

Holcolm nodded eagerly and drew back on his reins as he readied the team for the turn. Hawk and Tames Horses dismounted. The two men stood beside the trail, watching as each wagon, washed clean of snow by the heavy rain, turned one by one onto the benchland. Each driver was smiling in weary relief as they rumbled on past Hawk and Tames Horses.

When every wagon had been accounted for, Hawk and Tames Horses mounted up and followed them onto the benchland. If Hawk was any judge, after much-needed sleep and recuperation, there would be a proper celebration. The settlers would send out hunting parties to bring in fresh meat, warm fires would be built to roast the venison, and the Quaker fiddlers would have everyone jumping to their scratchy tunes.

They had good reason to celebrate. They had made it safely into their new land, foiling renegade white men, Blackfoot attacks, and at the last of it, the worst that Mother Nature could throw at them.

A week later, with the Blue Mountains at their backs, the wagon train reached a crossroads in the trail. The wagons halted. The journey from this point on would take the settlers almost due north to the Willamette Valley, while Hawk and Tames Horses would continue straight on to the coast as they searched for Bannister and a ship captain willing to take on board stolen furs and stolen women.

Hawk and Tames Horses had just about finished with their good-byes, a formality they had no wish to hurry. They had come to respect deeply these settlers and the pious, kindly Quakers. What to

Hawk had proven even more endearing than the Quakers' unbending, almost inflexible kindness was their humanity; they were as quirky and as prone to error as the rest of humankind, but as their battle with the Blackfoot proved, when the chips were down, they knew how to fight as well as any pioneer.

"Before you go, Hawk," Caleb Tribe said as he finished wringing Hawk's hand, "I want you to speak to old Elias."

"Why?"

"You're going after Bannister, aren't you?"

"You know we are."

"I think he might be able to help you."

"You mean he knows something?"

"That's the problem. I think he does. And so does he. But he's got such a terrible memory, he doesn't like to admit it. He thinks he might have heard something you could use."

"What did he hear?"

"He thinks he overheard Bannister mention where he was going to meet that ship's captain."

"Why the hell didn't you tell me this sooner, Caleb?"

"Now, don't get your dander up. The thing is if you ask him outright, he's liable to deny he heard anything. Sarah says it's at the tip of his tongue, but every time he tries to recall what he heard exactly, it slips away from him. And he vows there's no sense in sending you on a wild-goose chase if he's got it all wrong."

"I'd prefer he let me be the judge of that."

"That's what I told Sarah. Them two are mighty grateful to you and Tames Horses for helping them get across that stream. Maybe when you say good-bye, you just might be able to nudge it out of Elias. Just be careful, though. He's a crotchety old geezer."

Hawk chuckled. "Thanks, Caleb. Leave it to me."

Elias was standing with Sarah in front of his wagon. Despite what he had been through, he looked fine, as did Sarah waiting beside him. A man who refused to admit his age, he was as spare as a rake handle with a thick thatch of pure white hair and a drooping mustache as clean as the driven snow. His lean, lantern-jawed face creased into a grin as Hawk neared him.

"Never thought we'd get past them Blackfoot or that storm, Hawk," he said, shaking his hand vigorously. "And when you shot off that cannon in the middle of that river, you near made me jump into the water myself."

"Land sakes," Sarah seconded eagerly. "I thought we was all going to drown."

"Maybe you can return the favor, Elias."

"Why, sure, Hawk. What can I do for you?"

"You overheard something maybe—where Bannister might be heading. That right?"

Elias frowned and glanced unhappily at Sarah. "Now, Hawk, I ain't sure. That's the pure and simple truth of it. I might've heard wrong, considering the condition I was in at that time, piled into that wagon with them women outside screeching somethin' awful as the Blackfoot took them off."

"I realize you're not certain what you heard, Elias. But anything at all would be a help—anything."

Elias took a deep breath. "Well, I did hear mention of that Chinese city, Shanghai."

"Shanghai?"

"That's right. Don't know why they'd be talking about that place, unless they was thinking of sailing there."

"Go on, Elias. What else did you hear?"

"Nothin' much. Said they was going to rove. I remember that."

"Rove?"

"Yup. Then they mentioned a tavern. Book Tavern, I think."

"Book Tavern?"

Elias nodded doubtfully. "That's right. Don't make no sense, does it, Jed. I don't think that devil Bannister could read nary a word. And it sure don't figure he'd be one to spend his time in a tavern reading books. Not that one." Elias shrugged. "I knowed none of this would help any, Jed, so I just kept my mouth shut. Didn't want to send you off on a wild goose chase."

Hawk was as puzzled as Elias. "That's all you heard?"

Elias nodded. "Bannister and his men moved off right after that."

"Well, thanks anyway, Elias. Maybe it'll make sense when I get a chance to think on it."

"Wish I could've been more help."

"You did fine, Elias. Just make it a safe trip now. The Willamette Valley isn't that far, I hear."

Elias grinned. "It better not be."

Hawk shook Elias' hand once more, touched his hat brim to Sarah, and stepped back to watch as Elias clambered up onto their wagon's high perch and unwound the reins from the brake lever. Sarah got up beside him and snatched up the horsewhip.

Holcolm called out to the settlers to make ready to pull out. Then he yelled, "Wagons ho!"

Moving back off the trail, Hawk waved as the whips cracked up and down the line. Traces groaned and leather squeaked as the wagon train creaked into motion. Tames Horses strode over to join Hawk and both waved good-bye. In a surprisingly short time the last wagon had vanished beyond the curve of a pine-covered foothill.

It was close to the end of a long day when Hawk and Tames Horses approached a settler's cabin. Built on a dreary flat, the cabin and barn were perched beside a thin stream that cut through the center of the flat. They had been climbing steadily throughout the day, and at this altitude Hawk could see how thin the soil was and how shallow-rooted the grass, a poverty of location amply symbolized by the settler's homestead.

The one-room cabin was ringed with pine stumps. Its roof was of sod squares, its ridgepole sagging. The privy sat crookedly behind the cabin on an uneven hole dug halfheartedly out of the stony soil. The front yard was littered with junk: a rusted hay mower, a rotting mattress, the broken, weed-infested bed of an abandoned farm wagon, and an overturned grindstone. Only the tall pole barn seemed the result of any solid, determined effort on the settler's part.

As they rode into the yard, a flock of chickens scattered, cackling indignantly. A dispirited collie left the barn, watched them sullenly for a moment, then flopped down to nip at fleas. The settler appeared on his porch, carrying a rifle, and a moment later his woman appeared in the open doorway behind him. She was an enormous, lank-haired Indian woman, of a tribe unknown to Hawk.

Hawk pulled up his black and waited for the settler to lower the rifle's long barrel. Beside Hawk, Tames Horses muttered something in Nez Percé. Hawk agreed with his companion. He too was not impressed, either by the settler or by his woman.

"Howdy, mister," Hawk said to the settler.

"Hello, yourself," he replied.

Hawk then touched his hat brim to the man's wife. She said something to her husband Hawk could not catch, and vanished back into the cabin.

"Just passing on by," said Hawk. "Me and Tames Horses. Been long day."

The fellow regarded them sourly. His sunken cheeks and cadaverous frame bore mute testimony to his lack of success in this region. But his eyes were sharp and alert. And mean.

"You're both welcome to any water," he announced, his voice grating and harsh. "And there's grain for your hosses in the barn. My woman's got some roots on the stove, if you've a mind to light and set a spell."

"Much obliged," Hawk told him.

"See to your hosses, then. I'll tell my woman to set two more places at the table." He turned and went back inside.

Hawk looked at Tames Horses. The Indian did not look very happy at the prospect of supper inside the cramped, mean-looking cabin.

"I think I will stay outside," he told Hawk.

"Can't do that. Wouldn't be right to turn down

their hospitality. They might take it the wrong way."

With a sigh, Tames Horses dismounted. Hawk did also and they led their horses toward the barn.

The smell that greeted Hawk when he entered the cabin almost knocked him back out the door. The interior of the place was dim, lit by only a single oil lamp hung from a sagging rafter. It took a moment for Hawk's stomach to accept the incredible stench. It was compounded of unwashed bodies, rotting swill, and carelessly emptied slops jars. A glance back at Tames Horses following in after him showed that the Indian was equally dismayed.

The settler was wearing a filthy cotton undershirt, bib overalls, and mud-encrusted, ankle-high farm boots. His hair was graying and wild. His woman's swollen bulk was covered by a formless gray sack of a dress, its sash hanging untied at her sides.

On the other side of the wood stove stood a tall, slim girl in her twenties, her black hair hanging in two massive braids across her full breasts. She wore a stained buckskin dress. Most of its fringes were missing and the skirt was shiny with grease. Through a long tear in one side of the skirt, Hawk glimpsed a portion of dusky thigh. On her feet were ragged moccasins a few inches too big for her. They were obvious hand-me-downs from her mother, Hawk realized.

"I'm Matt Flemm," the settler said, shaking Hawk's hand and doing his best to ignore Tames Horses' impassive stare. "This here's my wife, Mountain Flower." He winked broadly at Hawk. "I just call her Mountain now."

Hawk nodded to Mountain Flower.

"And that's my daughter over there, Mary Jane."

Hawk introduced himself and Tames Horses to them, then sat down at the bench that served as a table. As the settler sat across from them and leaned close, the smell of his unwashed body smote Hawk's senses. Hawk had washed himself as thoroughly as he could at the pump outside, but it was obvious the settler was unconscious of the necessity for such ablutions and was waiting for next spring before either peeling off and washing his clothes or getting himself wet.

The roots the settler had mentioned his wife was cooking turned out to be turnips and potatoes, simmering in a thick broth, with chunks of succulent meat swimming in it. Surprisingly delicious, it was a stew hearty enough to warm Hawk's insides, and Tames Horses appeared to be satisfied as well. But as Hawk spooned a second portion onto his plate, he was careful not to ask what kind of meat it was.

The settler and his wife ate with solemn intensity, their heads down, spooning the stew into their mouths at a prodigious rate, as if fearful someone would come along and snatch the bowl from them. They reminded Hawk of hogs at a trough. The girl, however, seemed more interested in Hawk than in the stew before her, glancing furtively across the table at him, her smoky eyes seeming to devour him.

When the meal was done, Flemm reached down for a jug of moonshine he kept between his legs and passed it across to Hawk. As Hawk lifted the jug, he took a sniff of the contents. The smell reminded him of a mildewed silo. Lifting the jug to his lips, he gulped down a hefty swallow, then blinked the tears from his eyes. It felt as if he had just swallowed a lighted kerosene lamp. Keeping his composure and ignoring the tiny beads of perspiration that popped out on his forehead, he passed the jug to Tames Horses.

"Hold it," Flemm cried, reaching across the table and snatching the jug from the Indian's hands. "I ain't never got no Indian drunk, and I don't aim to start now. We'll all be scalped in our beds."

Tames Horses stared with some amusement at Flemm; then, with a slight, barely perceptible smile on his face, he shrugged. "Maybe white chief right."

Hawk was in no condition to comment. His tonsils were on fire. Flemm lifted the jug high and took two prodigious gulps, his Adam's apple dancing happily. Then, wiping his mouth with the back of his hand, he passed the jug to Mountain Flower. She had been waiting impatiently. Grabbing it from her husband, she lifted her head back and took two long swallows, after which, pausing only long enough to wipe off her mouth, she raised the jug to her lips a second time.

But Flemm wouldn't allow it. He snatched the jug from her and slapped her face hard. "I told you, Injun! One swig is all you get!"

As he handed the jug to Mary Jane, Flemm grinned across the table at Hawk. "I don't dare let Mountain near this here jug, less'n we got guests. Like now. Her Injun blood sure as hell takes over when that firewater hits her gut, I can tell you." His eyes lit. "One night she came after me with a butcher knife and sliced off part of my ear." Leaning forward, he turned his head so Hawk and Tames Horses could see the damage. "Next day she didn't remember a thing about it."

As Mary Jane was about to take a second swig, Flemm pulled the jug out of her hand.

"That's enough for you two," Flemm told the two women, slapping the cork into the jug and placing it back down between his legs. "An if'n I catch either of you at this jug tonight, I'll whup you till yore tails drop off."

Mary Jane glared unhappily at Flemm for a moment, then looked away, at Hawk this time, her eyes glowing like those of a wildcat. The moonshine had set bells to ringing inside her head, Hawk realized. She was part Indian, after all.

Mountain Flower heaved herself to her feet and began clearing off the table. Without a word Mary Jane joined her.

Flemm peered at Hawk. "Where you headin', Jed?"

"Depends. I'm looking for someone."

"You a lawman?"

Hawk shook his head.

"Didn't think so. Never saw a lawman traveling with a redskin before."

"I'm looking for a man calls himself Judge Bannister. He'd be traveling with a cart filled with furs, heading for the coast."

"Never laid eyes on him."

Hawk didn't expect Bannister to follow exactly the same route to the coast Hawk was taking, but he had felt it would do no harm to inquire. Now that he had, he was anxious to leave the cabin. He

could feel the girl's eyes on him, the bold intent-
ness of her stare almost enough to force him to look
in her direction. When at last he did, she smiled,
revealing teeth that gleamed like a beacon in her
dusky face.

He got to his feet, his head brushing lightly against
the coal-oil lamp. There was, thankfully, no room
in the small cabin for Tames Horses and himself to
spend the night, not that Hawk would have allowed
himself to sleep there even if there had been room.
The smell of well-trampled horse manure and urine
was infinitely preferable to the cabin's awful stench.

"Guess we'll sleep out in the barn," he told
Flemm.

Mountain Flower spoke up for the first time.
"Mary Jane show you to the barn."

Hawk was about to protest that he could find it
all by himself, but swallowed the words when he
saw the sudden, eager glow in the girl's cheeks as
she brushed quickly past the table and led the way
out of the cabin.

Mary Jane lifted the lantern so its light carried.
"You like it over there?" she asked, pointing to a
corner of the barn piled with hay.

Hawk glanced at Tames Horses. "All right for
me. What about you, Tames Horses?"

"I sleep over there," the Indian replied, pointing
to a broken stall off to their right. It too was filled
with hay.

Hawk walked over and examined the corner Mary
Jane had indicated, the girl at his side. Satisfied, he
fetched his bedroll, opened the sugan, and spread it
on top of the hay. The hay was still curing and

smelling faintly of honeysuckle. As he opened up
the bedroll, Mary Jane hung the lantern on a nail
and dropped to her knees beside him to help. Their
hands brushed as they both reached for the sugan's
flap.

Her hand was on fire. He looked into her eyes.
They were smoldering. Hawk was on fire himself, but he could not forget how filthy her parents
were, how the stench in their cabin had nearly
turned his stomach. Though Mary Jane did not
smell at all bad, a faint wisp of her parents'
filthiness clung to her.

He stood up hastily. She stood up also and faced
him, her eyes glowing, waiting for him to take her
in his arms.

"I'm tired, Mary Jane," he told her lamely. "Exhausted. I will sure be glad to get some sleep."

He saw disappointment in her eyes, then anger.
"You do not want me tonight?"

He hated angering the girl, and he had no desire
to hurt her feelings. And over the years he had
learned that the only thing worse than taking a
woman against her will was not taking her when
this was what she wanted. But he had decided he
would not bed this young lady, and that was that.

He cleared his throat. "I admit, Mary Jane, that
would be nice, but not tonight. Some other time.
I'm just so damned tired. I don't think I could . . .
manage it." He shrugged and smiled helplessly.

She understood. Perfectly.

"All right," she said, lifting the lantern from the
nail. She turned away and left the barn.

Hawk sighed and snuggled into the sugan, wondering if he wasn't a damn fool, after all.

Before he was able to answer the question to his complete satisfaction, he dropped off. When he awoke, it was still night, a cool moonless night. He wasn't sure at first what had awakened him. Then he heard a soft, sibilant cry. It came from the mouth of a woman. It was Mary Jane, he realized. She was calling to him from outside the barn. He sat up quickly and peeled off his britches, then his long johns. His earlier reluctance to take the fiery young lady seemed now to have been the response of a churlish fool.

He waited. The tiny cry came again. Frowning, he flipped aside the sugan flap and stood up. When he heard the sound again, he padded carefully across the straw-littered floor to the stall Tames Horses had selected for his couch.

The old Nez Percé warrior was not alone.

Enough light filtered into the barn for Hawk to see Mary Jane's naked form crouched astride the old Indian. He was as naked as she was, a long, stringy, plucked chicken of a man. Her breasts glistened from the beads of moisture covering her body. Ignoring Hawk's presence, she continued her slow, careful thrusting, her head leaning back, her tongue flickering over her lips as she savored every measured stroke. Only once did she glance up at him, her eyes like burning coals.

Tames Horses turned his head to look at Hawk. "Sometimes," he said, "I think Golden Hawk is fool."

"You keep on like this, old man, your heart may give out."

Tames Horses regarded Mary Jane with affection, then reached up to cup her swaying breasts with his old hands. "It will be a good way to die," he murmured softly.

Hawk turned and went back to his sugan, trying to tell himself he did not begrudge the old Indian's good fortune.

Hawk awoke again that same night, much later, aroused this time by a familiar and noxious stench that threatened to overwhelm him. Opening his eyes, he saw Matt Flemm towering over him in the darkness, a knife gleaming in his right hand. A split second before it flashed down, Hawk rolled aside. The knife sliced down through the sugan, biting deep into the floorboard beneath it. Vaulting to his feet, Hawk caught Flemm in the midsection with his shoulder and smashed him violently back against the wall. Flemm gasped in surprise and pain. In Hawk's powerful grip, he lost all resolve. Twisting frantically away, he turned to flee from the barn. Hawk caught him from behind, spun him around, and flung him headfirst into the wall.

Flemm groaned, straightened, and moved groggily to face Hawk, holding both hands up to protect himself. Hawk punched through the man's weak defense, planting measured blows on the point of his jaw, slamming his head around into the wall with each punch. Desperate, Flemm came back at Hawk with a wild flurry of weak punches. Ignoring them, Hawk bored in relentlessly, pounding the man about the head and shoulders with metronomic precision, until at last it was only the wall behind Flemm that kept him upright.

Hawk stepped back and kicked Flemm in the ribs. He did it twice, with calm deliberateness. He was sure he heard a rib crack and moved away from the sagging figure. With nothing to hold him up, Flemm toppled facedown onto the barn floor. He landed so heavily he appeared to bounce.

A heavy figure appeared in the open barn doorway—Mountain Flower. The long barrel of her husband's rifle gleamed dully in her hand. Tames Horses materialized beside her and in a sudden, chopping motion brought his right hand down on the base of her neck. As Mountain Flower collapsed, the rifle detonated, sending its ball into the floor at Hawk's feet.

Outside the barn Hawk saw Mary Jane peering through the open doorway. There was a pistol in her hand.

"Hold it right there, Mary Jane," Hawk told her, dropping to the floor and snatching up Flemm's knife. "I'm holding a knife against your father's throat. Take another step and I'll slit it."

"Kill the bastard," she said, lowering her pistol and striding into the barn. She stepped over her mother's body and came to a halt beside Flemm, gazing with fine contempt at his sprawled figure. "I wasn't goin' to hurt you fellers none. I came out to warn you." She chuckled. "I reckon it weren't necessary."

Hawk stood up. "That's not a very nice way to talk about your father," he suggested.

"Hell! He ain't my father," she retorted. "And I don't rightly know who is. But I don't much care, just so long as it ain't this here son of a bitch. Good riddance, I say."

Tames Horses came over. Mary Jane turned at his approach and, remembering their recent happy

time, smiled warmly at him. A groan came from
Mountain Flower. They looked over at her. She
stirred groggily, then grabbed the barn door and
pulled her bulk upright.

She rubbed the back of her neck and looked with
amazement at her daughter. "Was that you hit me,
Mary Jane?"

"Nope. It was Tames Horses."

Squinting painfully, she looked over at Tames
Horses. "No need you do that," she complained. "I
just come with rifle to stop Matt. I know he cannot
get away with it. I tell him. Two men out here, and
one is an Indian."

"You were right, Mountain Flower," Hawk replied. "He didn't get away with it. You might tell
him to take a bath next time he decides to sneak up
on someone."

"He is one big smelly bastard, all right," she
agreed. "Now you soften him up good. Make it easy
for me to wash him off some." She smiled. "Maybe
I fill tub and give him bath."

"Why he want to kill us?" Tames Horses asked.

"He's after your horses and the Hawken rifle. He
spotted that right off."

Mary Jane spoke up. "Three men rode in a couple of days ago. They was lookin' for the same feller
you are."

"Bannister?"

"Yep," the girl said. "We fed them, like we did
you, made them real to home, and then the bastards
raped me and Ma, knocked Matt around some, and
took three of our best horses and Matt's rifle."

Hawk glanced down at the unconscious man. "So

Matt figured we were members of the same gang and decided to get even."

"Yes."

"Which way did they go?"

"To Pine Bluff."

"Which way's that?"

"It's on the other side of the pass."

"Maybe you can give me directions."

Mary Jane nodded quickly. "Don't see why not."

Hawk looked at Tames Horses. "Those three must be what was left of Bannister's crew, the ones who ran off when we took the fort back. Looks like we're heading in the right direction, anyway."

Matt Flemm groaned and began to stir. Mountain Flower waddled over, reached down, and with little apparent exertion, flung Matt Flemm's lank frame over her shoulder. She vanished with him out through the barn door.

Following after her mother, Mary Jane called back, "You two can go back to sleep now. Matt won't be botherin' you no more."

The next morning Hawk and Tames Horses had already saddled up and were about ready to ride out when Mary Jane appeared in the barn doorway to invite them in to breakfast.

The offer surprised Hawk, but he accepted for himself and Tames Horses, and a moment later, the two men entered the cabin warily and sat down. Hawk rested his loaded Hawken carefully on the table beside him. Matt Flemm was sitting up in a far corner, a dirty bandage wrapped around his face, his forehead swollen. Otherwise, he appeared to be reasonably fit. He scowled unhappily at Hawk.

"There weren't no need for you to get so riled up," he said. "It was them other gents what came along before you. They got me mad, they did, and I thought you was part of the same brood."

"You should've told me about them. I could've set you straight," Hawk told him.

"Yep. Should've done that, I reckon. You busted two of my ribs."

"And I did it on purpose, Flemm."

"I figured you did."

Mountain Flower put before them on the table an enormous platter of ham and eggs, garnished with a small mountain of fried potatoes as Mary Jane set clean dishes down in front of them. Then she poured their coffee and left the cabin. Mountain Flower sat down and with an almost fond regard watched them eat. But something Hawk had caught in Mary Jane's glance as she left the cabin bothered him.

"Where'd Mary Jane go?" he asked Mountain Flower nervously.

"To saddle up her horse."

Hawk frowned. "She goin' somewhere?"

"What's matter with you? She tell you already she show you way to Pine Bluff. Why you surprise?"

"Mary Jane doesn't have to ride along with us. She can just tell us how to get there."

"No. She want show you."

Tames Horses turned to look at Hawk. "Let her come. She fine young woman. She show us much. You see."

With a weary shrug Hawk set to work on his breakfast. The platter of food had shrunk noticeably. Tames Horses was way ahead of him. Last night's earlier activities seemed to have done great things for his appetite.

Drowning his breakfast with two final cups of coffee, Hawk left the cabin with Tames Horses. Mary Jane was already up on her horse waiting for them. She was astride a small powerful gray, and it looked as if she were ready for a long journey, with a fat bedroll tied snugly to her saddle's cantle and both saddlebags bulging. A wide, floppy-brimmed hat shaded most of her face.

Hawk and Tames Horses mounted up.

"So long, Ma," Mary Jane called to her mother who was watching from the porch. "Don't let that son of a bitch get behind you."

"Nope," Mountain Flower said, "I won't."

As the three riders pulled away from the porch and started from the yard, the big woman waved good-bye and slumped heavily down into a sagging wicker chair. Reaching under it, she produced Flemm's jug of moonshine and sat it up on her big lap, contented.

Riding out of the yard, Hawk glanced back. Mountain Flower's head was leaning far back, the jug standing straight up. It wouldn't be long before she emptied it.

Watch out, Matt Flemm.

—6—

At midday, two days later, they reached the Pacific and halted. Visible just beyond a low bluff, the water stretched as far as the eye could see, the sky blending imperceptibly into the hazy horizon. The sense of something vast and illimitable waiting before them was exciting. Hawk could smell the salt in the air.

He glanced at Tames Horses. The old Indian's eyes had lit at sight of the Pacific, and he sat his pony now, enormously impressed and pleased that he had come this far with Hawk to see this awesome sight. It was definitely not a letdown for him, Hawk was glad to see.

"Ain't Tames Horses never seen the ocean before?" Mary Jane asked Hawk.

"No, he hasn't. I haven't seen it before myself. Never came this far before. Cut back as soon as I got beyond the mountains."

"I seen it before," Mary Jane said. "It ain't so much."

"I guess that depends."

"On what?"

"On what you compare it with."

Hawk looked over at Tames Horses. "Ready?"

The old warrior nodded. "We go now. Later, I will stand in the water and let it wash over my feet."

Hawk chuckled and they started up again.

A half-hour later they approached a medium-sized herd of buffalo feeding on patches of thick, spongy grama grass. Most of the herd occupied a large, dry watercourse, but some of the massive, hunched beasts had ranged far from the herd, feasting in the hollows on tawny bluestem, some of it high enough to brush the belly of Hawk's black.

Hawk was closest to one old bull as they rode past. The big fellow turned to face him, lowered its head, and snorted some, its tiny ears fluttering. The black did not spook and Hawk kept to the same pace. The bull stood his ground and moved just enough to keep his eyes on Hawk. Riding alongside Hawk, Tames Horses looked the bull over admiringly.

"This is first time I hear of buffalo this side of the mountains," he remarked. "Maybe Blackfoot drive them here. Maybe now Nez Percé can hunt buffalo in this land. This is good thing."

"It's just a stray herd," Hawk replied. "I wouldn't count on it. It's too small a herd to last."

"Maybe so," Tames Horses agreed. "And maybe this Indian come back here and take down a fat cow." His eyes gleamed as he contemplated the hunt.

"Easy, Chief," Hawk told him gently. "We got other business in this land."

The Indian shrugged. It was clear Tames Horses would rather not dismiss such an exciting prospect that easily, but he rode on without further discussion of it. The buffalo herd was soon left behind.

They reached the town of Pine Bluff later that same day, clattering across a rough-plank bridge that spanned a shallow stream. Along the single Main Street were lined a half-dozen or so falsefront stores. A depressing number of them were out of business. An imposing brick hotel on the other end of town looked as if it had closed off its top third floor. The shades were drawn and the sunlight had faded them to a blank, staring white. Like the eyes of a dead man.

It was a town in trouble, obviously. The men lounging on the porch outside the only saloon reminded Hawk of vultures hunched on tree limbs. He rode on past the saloon without pause, feeling the eyes of the hard cases watching them. If this was where Bannister's men had come to roost, they had chosen wisely.

They kept on until they reached the hotel. It was called the St. James. Dismounting stiffly, Hawk dropped his reins over the hitch rail and waited for Tames Horses and Mary Jane to join him. Then they went inside. The desk clerk was a tall beanpole of a man with a prominent Adam's apple and beetling brows. He was dressed in an immaculate white cotton shirt and a dark frock coat. A black string tie was knotted at his throat.

Smoothing his thinning gray hair back with a long-fingered hand, he smiled cheerfully at Hawk. "Good afternoon," he said in a clipped British accent. "A room for the night?"

"That's right. One for me and Tames Horses here. And another for Mary Jane."

"You mean you will be sharing a room with an aborigine?"

"I am not aborigine," Tames Horses told the desk clerk solemnly. "I am Nez Percé."

The clerk smiled nervously. "It makes no difference. I am afraid there is a town ordinance forbidding this."

"Forbidding what?" Hawk demanded.

"Native aborigines—in this case a Nez Percé Indian—are not allowed to take a room in this hotel, or anywhere in the town, as I understand it."

"Who's going to enforce this ordinance?"

"Why, the town marshal, of course."

"You give us the rooms, we'll deal with the town marshal."

"I don't know if I should do that, sir—"

A girl stepped out of the office behind the desk. "Do it, Pa," she said.

She was in her late twenties and wore Levi's and a red cotton shirt. She was almost as tall as Hawk, and her eyes and the shape of her face confirmed her indisputably to be the desk clerk's daughter.

Her father twisted to face her. "But, Louise, you know the law. And you know what an animal the town marshal is. This will cause trouble."

"In this town, that's all we got, Pa," she remarked, moving up beside him and smiling at Hawk. "We got three payin' guests. That's the important thing."

With a sigh, her father dipped a quill pen into the inkwell, swiveled the register, and handed the pen to Hawk. Hawk signed the register, made a mark for Tames Horses, then handed the pen to Mary Jane.

"Make a mark for me too," she told Hawk.

Hawk traced a quick, five-pointed star in the registry, handed the pen back to the desk clerk, and turned the register back around.

The man glanced at the two marks. "Most unusual," he sighed, reaching back for the keys.

On the second floor, when Hawk gave a room key to Mary Jane, she said, "I'll be bunkin' with Tames Horses, Jed. You kin have that room to yourself."

Hawk glanced at Tames Horses.

The Indian shrugged.

Hawk did not argue.

When he went downstairs a moment later to see to his horse and bring up his gear, he found Louise manning the front desk.

"Is there a stable nearby?"

"The hotel has one. In back. Bring your horses around and I'll tend to them."

"No stable boy?"

"You're lookin' at him."

"Times are hard."

"You got it right, Mr. Thompson."

"I'd like to thank you. I hope letting Tames Horses take a room here won't cause you any trouble."

"If it does, we can handle it." She reached under the desk and brought up a sawed-off shotgun. "It's loaded with double-ought-six, and everyone in town knows I can use it."

"I hope it won't come to that. Where can I get a bath, shave, and a haircut?"

"Burt Physer's barber shop. Across the street. He

doesn't have much call for baths. Not in this town. But he'll be able to take care of you."

"Much obliged, Miss . . ."

"Burton. Louise Burton. My father's Ronald. He doesn't like that town ordinance any more than I do, Mr. Thompson, but he's got some notion he wants to keep me out of trouble and figures the best way is not to stir up the town marshal."

"I can understand his concern."

Hawk touched his hat brim to her and went outside for the horses. When he led them around back to the stable, Louise was standing in the barn's doorway, waiting for him. He watched her as she led his black into a stall. Her movements were deft and gentle as she lifted the saddle from the steaming black's back and parked it astride the stall's partition. Confident she knew what she was doing, he hefted his saddle roll and saddlebags over his shoulders, grabbed his rifle, and went back upstairs.

On the way to his room he paused by Tames Horses' door, heard soft, pleasant sounds coming from within, smiled, and ducked into his own room. Not long after, he crossed the street to the barber shop and caught the barber dozing in one of his chairs.

Burt Physer was a short, jowly man with a pleasant smile. He was more than generous with the hot water he poured into the large, enameled tub Hawk used in the back room. After lazing in the tub for a full half-hour, Hawk dressed in fresh buckskins and let Burt shave him.

During the shave, Hawk got a line on the town.

Ronald Burton and his daughter ran the hotel alone. Burton had once been a high official in Hudson's Bay Company, and rumor had it that when he saw how swiftly and completely the company was losing its influence in the Northwest fur trade, he had packed it in and purchased the hotel with his life savings. As luck would have it, no sooner had Burton bought the hotel than settlers began bypassing the coast, heading directly either for the land around Oregon City or for the Willamette Valley. The general store, a mill, and a blacksmith shop had since been abandoned, leaving the town to exist on the few settlers who still came through from California on their way north to Seattle. Recently, an increasing number of gunslicks had been drifting in.

"What's keepin' them alive?"

"Smuggling."

"You sure of that?"

Physer chuckled. "I can always tell when a ship hits the coast. All of a sudden there's plenty of money in town, most of which is spent in the saloon."

"What are they smuggling?"

Burt Physer had finished shaving Hawk and was now trimming his hair. He stepped back, flexing the scissors cheerfully, and pursed his lips. "Don't think I want to go into that, mister."

"Why not?"

"I'm not sure. And maybe I've already told you too much."

"Maybe I ought to go see the town marshal."

"You a lawman?"

"Nope."

"Didn't think so. Not many lawmen ride in with a Nez Percé Indian and a white girl astride a buckskin." Physer put away his scissors, brushed perfumed powder over Hawk, then peeled off the striped sheet, snapping it for emphasis. "Shave, haircut, and a bath. That'll be two bits, mister."

Hawk dropped the coins into the barber's waiting palm. "Ever hear of a man called Bannister? Judge Bannister?"

"Sure. He's the one who owns the town marshal."

"Where can I find him?"

"Beats the shit out of me. He's been and gone. Hard to get that man to light."

"Thanks, Burt."

"Mister, anything I told you, you never heard from me."

Hawk nodded. He understood perfectly.

Louise Burton was back manning the front desk when Hawk returned to the hotel. She looked up brightly as he approached, and smiled. "If you're hungry," she said, "I'd be glad to fix something. We don't have a menu, there are so few travelers lately."

"Steak and fixings would be fine," Hawk told her.

"It won't be a minute. Go on into the dining room and find a table. Sit anywhere you want. It won't matter."

"I was going to go on up and check on my two partners."

"The Nez Percé and the girl?"

He nodded.

"I'm afraid they've already left. The Indian asked where you'd gone and I told him I thought you'd gone over to the barber shop to get a bath. Then he asked how far the ocean was. It's not far, so I told him. I know this sounds funny, but I think he and the girl are going to take a bath in the Pacific. Could that be possible?"

Hawk laughed. "Yes, it could—and a damned good idea. That Indian's come a long ways to see the ocean."

Hawk stepped into the dining room and found a table near a window. Louise hurried out of the kitchen with silverware and fresh linen. As she poured him a glass of water, he glanced up at her.

"Why not join me?" he said. "I'd appreciate your company. Your father could hold down the front desk, couldn't he?"

She blushed. "If you wish."

"Fine."

The meal was served with astonishingly little delay. Louise brought in a platter holding a two-inch-thick steak. Alongside it she placed a bowl of mashed potatoes, gravy, a plate of still-warm bread cut in thick slices, and a saucer of freshly churned butter. The steaming coffee had plenty of cream and honey to go with it. After Louise set a fresh pot of coffee down before him, she sat across from him, content with a modest portion of steak and one helping of potato.

They chatted pleasantly enough through the meal. Louise did her best to hide her amazement, if not her interest, when in answer to one of her questions Hawk revealed that he had spent a long stretch of his youth as a member of the Antelope Comanches. He went on to mention that he had visited his sister on the East Coast of the United States, yet was now a perfectly content mountain man and occasional guide for settlers who found it not a bit unusual to take an Indian woman for a wife.

"And now you've come here looking for Bannister."

"That's right," Hawk replied, and told her why.

Her face was pale when he had finished. "Well, at least the settlers are safe now."

"Yes. Now all I have to do is find Bannister—and Sam Baldwin and his sister."

"You and that Indian have come a long way."

Hawk shrugged.

"And you've had so many adventures."

"I once thought I would keep a journal—write it all down. And for a while I did. But I gave it up. I don't think anyone would believe it, anyway."

She laughed. "Perhaps you're right." Then she glanced down at his empty cup. "Would you like a glass of beer?"

"Sounds good."

"I'll join you in one myself, if you don't mind."

"By all means."

When she had rejoined him, a stein of beer sitting in front of them both, Louise told Hawk what she knew. There had been talk for months that oceangoing, sailing vessels had been putting in along the coast somewhere. They were smuggling in contraband and taking on crews and furs in exchange. The problem, it seems, was that the ship captains couldn't keep their seamen on board once they put into San Francisco. The gold fever was too great. The city was going wild and people were pouring into California from all over the world to head for the goldfields.

Hawk nodded. This news did not make him happy, especially when he thought of his sister Annabelle and her husband. He knew it would change things in California drastically, and from the letters he had gotten from his sister, he could tell it already had. Gold had a way of driving men mad. It was something he knew from bitter personal experience.

"Anyway," Louise went on, "these captains need crews."

"But where do they get them? There aren't that many seamen in this wilderness."

"Have you ever heard of shanghaiing?"

Hawk frowned, suddenly remembering old Elias Smithers and his creaky memory. Elias said he had heard Bannister discussing the Chinese city of Shanghai, but what he had actually heard, Hawk realized now, was a discussion of the brutal practice of shanghaiing. In the Boston port Hawk had heard the term often.

"Yes, Louise," he said. "I've heard of that."

"And you know what it means?"

"It means drugging men, then kidnapping them and forcing them to serve as crewmen aboard ships bound for the Orient. Though they know little or nothing about ships or the sea, under the lash they learn quickly."

Louise nodded bleakly. "Well, that's what's going on, then. That's what Bannister is doing. He's supplying ships with crews, just as you described."

"Where's he getting the men?"

"Usually from local Indians tribes, I'm afraid."

"Which ones?"

"Mostly the Tillamook and Tolowa."

"Haven't heard much of those Indians."

"And you won't, either. First it was smallpox, and since then rum and tuberculosis and other diseases, too filthy to mention. The worst part of it is, these Indians are selling some of their own people to Bannister, sometimes for only a few barrels of liquor."

"They probably throw in furs, too."

"Yes, that too. Did you know that Bannister used to work for the Hudson's Bay Company? My father fired him years ago." She shuddered. "As you can imagine, that hasn't made it any easier for us here."

"Has Bannister been giving your father trouble?"

"Not directly. We hardly ever see him. But he doesn't have to be here to make his presence felt. He's made it impossible for us to prosper as his cutthroats take over this town, while at the same time he refuses to let my father sell out."

"How can he do that?"

"By simply terrifying any potential buyer half to death. It's most effective, I can tell you."

"He does that?"

"No. His bully boys. The town marshal, for one."

"What's his name?"

"Monk Cahill."

"He wear a star?"

"Yes. Of course, it means absolutely nothing."

Hawk didn't need to be told that. "Louise, I followed three men to this town. Men who worked for Bannister at that fort he took over on the other side of the mountains. Have you noticed any new faces in town?"

"I try not to," she said.

"Where would I look? I figure they might be able to lead me to Bannister."

"The saloon. It's their hangout."

"That's about what I figured."

"So you'll be going over there," she sighed.

"That's right."

"You're just one man, you know."

"I'll ask a few questions, stir up the pot some, see what boils up."

"You sound like you know what you're doing. But be careful, Jed. These are not very nice men."

"I don't expect they are. But I'll be careful."

"Promise?"

"I promise."

They finished their beers. Hawk paid up and thanked Louise. In his room, he checked the load in his Walker, patted the knife Tames Horses had given him, then went back downstairs. It was almost dark when he stepped up onto the saloon's low porch.

Pushing through the batwings, he looked the place over. As the only real going business in town, the saloon was busy enough. Its floor was covered with sawdust that had not been swamped for weeks. The spittoons were overflowing with tobacco juice. Thick tendrils of smoke hung in blue layers about the tables and chairs, partially obscuring the kerosene lamps hanging from the ceilings and the long mirror behind the bar. The smell of unwashed feet and cheap cigars was heavy in the place.

Three bar girls—dressed in short, faded blue dresses—turned to look at him as he stood by the entrance. They were Indian girls, probably from the tribes Louise had mentioned. One of them was barely in her teens and had more than likely been sold to the saloon's owner for not much more than an ancient flintlock and a few ratty blankets. Despite their gaudy dress, the girls looked drawn and forlorn, like children who had long since given up trying to escape a nightmare. One of them, the youngest, had stuck a wildflower in her hair. It had long since wilted.

As Hawk stood by the doorway, the sound of the doors flipping shut behind him sounded clearly in the waiting silence. There couldn't be a man in the place, he realized, who had not heard of him and his two companions riding into town that afternoon, and if the three he had tracked this far had seen him as well, they would know for sure who he was after.

Hawk walked over to the bar and elbowed past the crush. "Whiskey," he told the barkeep, a round man with a flat, porcine nose.

He slapped a bottle of whiskey and a shot glass down on the bar.

Hawk paid him and took the bottle and glass over to a table in a corner of the room. Sitting with his back to the wall, he filled the shot glass and downed it, then looked around.

He had no difficulty picking out the town marshal. Monk Cahill's greasy star shone dully in the dim light. He was playing poker at a table not far from Hawk's. The town marshal was aptly named. There was a definite simian cast to his powerful, thickset frame. His eyes were small and sharp, peering at the cards in his hand from under formidable brows. His arms seemed overlong, his ridged knuckles hairy, and when he spoke, it was like the bark of an angry animal. The men crowding about to watch the poker game treated him with a sickening, abject subservience.

The saloon's patrons were an odd lot. Most wore

the wool knit hats and the black wool jackets favored by seamen. Instead of boots, they wore ankle-high seamen's shoes, and from their mouths came salty oaths and nautical terms Hawk remembered dimly having heard years before when visiting the Boston seaport.

Hawk was reaching for his bottle when a sharp cry came from his right.

He glanced over. A scrawny redhead in a ragged wool cap had just cuffed one of the Indian bar girls. The force of the blow had spun her head around. The girl's eyes were shut and she was trying not to cry, but tears were already moving down her cheeks. Her spirit broken, she allowed the seaman to pull her roughly down onto his lap.

"That's the way, Red," someone cried. "She's just your size."

"You bet," he said.

Hawk had seen the man before. He was sure of it. He turned slightly in his chair to get a better look at him. The seaman caught the movement and stared back at Hawk, his eyes suddenly mean, challenging. He no longer seemed interested in the bar girl.

At once Hawk remembered where he had seen him before. When Bannister had taken him captive, this was the worthy who had reached over and taken Hawk's Walker Colt. Johnny Bear had retrieved it not long after that, somehow, enabling Hawk to regain the Colt when he killed the Blackfoot.

The scrawny redhead pushed the Indian girl off his lap and stood up to face Hawk.

"I know you," he said, starting slowly toward Hawk. Monk Cahill tossed aside his hand to watch the action, as did the rest of the saloon's patrons.

"You're that bloke they call Hawk. It was you helped them damned settlers take the fort back and massacre our crew."

Hawk didn't think it necessary to reply.

"You been followin' us, ain't you?"

Hawk shrugged. "Maybe so."

"You're damned right." His eyes fastened on the Walker Colt in Hawk's belt. "I see you took the Colt back from that goddamn Blackfoot who took it from me."

Hawk nodded.

"It was Bannister made me give it to Johnny Bear. I figure it's really mine. I want it."

"Then come and take it."

As Hawk spoke, he got to his feet, keeping the table between them. Red pulled up warily, his icy-green eyes murderous. His hand dropped to the pistol in his belt. As he drew it, Hawk pushed his foot against the table and jammed it into Red's midsection, driving him violently back. The table's edge almost cut the scrawny man in half as it smashed him against the wall. Red gasped painfully and dropped his pistol.

Reaching over the table with both hands, Hawk yanked the man out from behind it and flung him bodily across the saloon. Red spun once, lost his balance, and reeled backward into the bar. As he tried to catch himself, his feet got tangled in the brass foot rail. Twisting painfully, he went down. Before he could recover, Hawk strode over and stomped on his right wrist. The sound of bone crunching under his heel filled the shocked saloon. As the little redhead, writhing in agony, clung to his shattered wrist, Hawk turned to face the others.

"Which one is next?"

Cahill was on his feet, knees bent, his simian body in a half-crouch. He was the only one in the place with a Paterson Colt strapped to his thigh. "What the hell do you want here, mister?" he asked. "I seen you and that Indian ride in. And that slut."

"You heard what Red said. I followed him and two others to this town."

"Why?"

"I'm looking for Bannister."

"He ain't here."

"Well, maybe he will be."

"You plan to wait for him, do you?" Cahill's eyes grew crafty.

"If that's what it takes."

Beside Hawk on the filthy, sawdust-covered floor, the redhead, half out of his mind with pain, squirmed and swore. He was like an injured animal, his eyes wild, his teeth gnashing. One of the bar girls hurried to his side. He spat at her venomously, but she persisted. Another joined her and together they dragged the mewling sailor the length of the bar, out of harm's way.

"Look," said Cahill reasonably. "I ain't got nothin' agin you. If you just came on board to wait for Bannister, that's no skin off my nose. But my advice to you is don't wait. Ride out while you still can."

"You mean after what I just done to your friend here, you'll let me ride out?"

"Like I told you, I ain't got no quarrel with you. We all saw what happened. Why, it's clear as spring water Red Christie started the whole thing." Cahill glanced at the two men siding him. "Ain't that right, mates?"

"Sure," the one nearest Cahill agreed. But he and his pal remained alert, their gun hands hovering inches above the pistols stuck in their belts.

Hawk smiled and waited.

It didn't take long. Cahill's hand dropped to the Colt on his thigh. Hawk drew his own weapon so swiftly that as he lifted his Colt from its holster, Cahill found himself staring into the enormous bore of Hawk's Walker. Cahill's face went slack. All bloodthirsty enthusiasm drained from it, and a calculating, respectful look entered his eyes, The two beside him straightened up swiftly and took hasty steps back.

Slowly, carefully, Cahill let his Colt slip back into its holster.

"That's better," said Hawk. "Now, where's Bannister?"

"Hell," said Cahill, swallowing uneasily, "I ain't his keeper."

Out of the corner of his eye, Hawk saw the barkeep's shoulder dip as he reached under the bar for his shotgun. Hawk swung his Colt around and fired. The man's flat, piggish nose became a bloody hole into which the rest of his face vanished as the back of his head exploded onto the mirror behind him. The sawed-off shotgun clattered across the polished surface of the bar and crashed to the floor.

Hawk spun back around. A small, ferret-faced man had drawn an ancient pistol. He fired hastily. As the round shattered the mirror behind him, Hawk fired back, thumb-cocked, and fired again.

Both rounds caught the little man squarely in his

chest, slamming him back sharply against a table. Dropping his pistol, the fellow collapsed slowly forward onto another table, rolled off it, and thudded heavily to the floor.

Not a man moved to help him.

Through the thick clouds of acrid gunsmoke, Hawk leveled his Walker at Monk Cahill. "One more time, Cahill," Hawk told him. "Where can I find Bannister?"

"Jesus, man, I don't know. He could be anywhere along the coast."

"Who's the ship captain he's dealing with?"

The man moistened his lips. Sweat stood out on his forehead. Hawk cocked his weapon and steadied it. Beside Cahill on the floor, the dying man was twisting slowly, groaning faintly. He was a reminder of what might lie in store.

"I'm waiting, Cahill," Hawk told him softly.

"The captain's name is Sutherland."

"And the name of his ship?"

"The *China Queen*."

His Colt still covering Cahill, Hawk strode from the saloon. When he reached the batwings and stepped out into the night, he heard the rush of feet stampeding toward the entrance. Turning, he fired two quick shots through the flimsy batwings. The rush halted and the saloon became very still.

As Hawk walked off, someone on the floor behind the batwings began to curse softly, bitterly.

Louise was standing in front of the hotel. She had heard the shooting.

"Are you all right, Jed?"

"So far," he said.

"From what I could hear, you did indeed stir the pot some."

Smiling, Hawk glanced back down the street at the saloon. The porch in front of it was crowded with men staring toward the hotel.

Ronald Burton marched from the hotel, a sawed-off shotgun in his hand. "I hear you're having trouble with the locals," he said grimly.

"You could say that," Hawk replied.

"I don't think it's going to be very healthy for you and your friends in this town," Burton sighed. "And that's too bad. It isn't often we get anyone here willing to stand up to those blackguards."

"Do you think you could keep an eye out down here while I go up for my gear?"

The man's eyes lit at the prospect. "You may go up to your room in perfect confidence," he said, patting the shotgun affectionately. "I welcome the opportunity to use this weapon. Indeed, I would say it is about time."

"I'll get your horse ready," Louise told him.

Hawk hurried into the hotel and up the stairs to the second floor. He rapped firmly on Tames Horses' door. When there was no response, he turned the knob and pushed the door open. The room was empty. Mary Jane and Tames Horses' gear lay strewn about the floor and piled in corners. They had not come back yet, it seemed.

Hawk didn't like it. They had gone for a swim in the Pacific. Like crazy kids. Thinking of Tames Horses, he knew for sure there was no fool like an old fool. The ocean was not that far, and it was night already. They should have been back by now—unless the old Nez Percé warrior on his way back had decided to find that buffalo herd and shoot himself a cow.

No. That was too crazy.

Hawk entered his own room, gathered his gear, and hurried down the back stairs to the stable. Leaving the gear with Louise, who was busy saddling his black, he returned to his room and bunched up his bedclothes to make it appear he was asleep in bed. The moonlight filtering through the window helped the deception considerably. Then he jammed the back of a chair up against the doorknob, opened the window, and climbed onto the livery's roof. Dropping lightly to the ground, he entered the barn.

Louise was waiting for him, holding the black's bridle. The horse was saddled, his gear tied on.

"Thanks," he told her.

"You better hurry," she replied. "If I know that crowd, you don't have much time."

He swung aboard the black and gathered up the reins. "I'm worried about Tames Horses and the girl. If they come back, tell them I'm heading for the coast. Tell them I'm looking for a ship called the *China Queen*."

She nodded quickly. "I'll tell them."

"If they don't come back, save their gear, will you? I'll be back for it."

"Yes." She stepped back. "Now, hurry."

Hawk ducked his head and rode out of the livery stable.

Keeping to the alley that ran behind the hotel, he soon quit the town and lifted the black to a lope as he made for a pine bluff looming into the night sky behind the town. Cresting it, he pulled the black to a halt to let it blow. As far as he could see, the fields below him were awash in moonlight, the roofs of the town silver in its glow.

From below he heard the faint popping of gunfire, punctuated by the roar of a shotgun. The breeze shifted and he heard nothing more. He sat his mount patiently. The gunfire must have come from men breaking into his room, he realized, and the shotgun would have been Ronald Burton making good on his promise. He hoped he and his daughter were not hurt. Dragging them into this had not been his intention.

A lone rider galloped out of town. From the way his chunky figure was bent over his horse, it was clear who it was: Monk Cahill. The town marshal was heading for the coast to warn someone.

Hawk was pleased—and not the least bit surprised.

Nudging the black off the bluff, Hawk angled down the steep grade, his eyes on the man who was going to lead him to Captain Sutherland of the *China Queen*.

And where Captain Sutherland was, Bannister could not be far behind.

Cahill reached the coast a little after midnight and camped high on a promontory overlooking the Pacific. Hawk made a dry camp well back from the water in sight of his campfire. Up at dawn, Cahill continued south along the coast until, a little before noon, he reached a steep bluff overlooking a cove. On the crest of the bluff, barely visible to Hawk through a thick stand of pine, there was a long, rambling warehouse, and it was toward this that Cahill rode. As Hawk followed Cahill's trail along the edge of the bluff, he saw far below him, jutting out from a rocky headland, a dock that he judged might be able to handle a good-sized lifeboat or even a small sailing vessel, but not an oceangoing merchantman or clipper ship.

Ahead of him, Cahill disappeared into the pines. Hawk followed him in, keeping his head low and being very careful. Emerging from the trees a moment or so later, he saw no sign of Cahill. The warehouse was clearly visible on the other side of the flat ahead of him. If Cahill had been heading for the warehouse, he should still have been riding across the meadow toward it. Hawk looked uneasily to his right, toward the ocean, then scanned the pines behind him. Nothing. No sign of Cahill. No movement.

He looked back at the warehouse. No one was entering or leaving it. The large double doors were firmly shut. The only windows were set at the top of the storehouse. A steep, wooded slope towered behind the building, which struck Hawk as a flimsy, makeshift structure. Warped, weathered boards covered the frame with little overlap and no real attempt to make the walls solid. A horse barn and corral were stationed behind it, close under the slope.

Pulling back into the pines, Hawk kept in their cover as he circled the flat, his eyes never leaving the warehouse. He was almost behind it when he caught some movement finally—two horses swishing their tails in the corral next to the horse barn. Passing, he hoped for more movement, some sign of human life.

It was then that he thought he heard something coming from the warehouse—a kind of dim wailing, or was it singing? Or were those cries, disjointed, desperate? The wind shifted. Now the only sound was the smash of the surf on the rocks far below and the occasional cry of a gull.

Hawk moved until he was as close as he could get to the warehouse without leaving the cover afforded by the timber. The slope loomed over him by this time, blocking the direct rays of the sun. He sent the horse out of the pines and headed for the horse barn.

Abruptly, a rifle shot rang out from the slope

behind him. The round came close, and it brought Hawk's every sense alert. He flung his black around and charged toward the slope. He had caught the flash of gunpowder. It came from a ledge marked by a tall pine. Another shot rang out. This one caught the black in the chest. As the animal crashed to the ground, Hawk was thrown clear.

Another round exploded the ground inches from his head. Colt in hand, he leapt to his feet, raced for the slope's cover, and scrambled up its steep incline. Twenty yards or so farther on, he broke into a clearing and peered anxiously through the trees above him. The tall pine marking the ledge was still visible off to his right. He concentrated then on clawing his way up the steep, needle-slick ground toward it.

He was within a few yards of it when he saw Cahill through the trees. The man was down on one knee, his rifle up to his shoulder, its muzzle staring down Hawk's throat. Hawk flung himself to one side a split second before Cahill fired. The slug clipped a pine over Hawk's head, showering its seeds over him. Flinging up his Colt, Hawk squeezed off a shot. The rifle in Cahill's hand bucked violently upward and out of Cahill's grasp.

Scrambling up the slope toward him, Hawk reached the ledge in time to see Cahill ducking behind a tree. Hawk snapped off two quick shots. One slug gouged a chunk of bark out of the tree. The other whined off a boulder farther on. Hawk held up momentarily, chiding himself. He usually hit what he aimed at, but he was winded from the steep climb, and he had no business trying to shoot a man he could no longer see.

Racing toward the tree behind which Cahill had vanished, he saw his quarry darting across a small clearing, heading for cover in the timber beyond. Hawk stopped and fired at Cahill with greater deliberation than before. Cahill spun to the ground, grabbing at his right side. But immediately he regained his feet and ducked into the trees.

Hawk slipped warily into the timber after him. Like any hurt animal, Cahill was now doubly dangerous. And Cahill was no man to mess with, Hawk realized as he held up on the edge of another small clearing and listened for any sound left by the fleeing man. A twig snapped to Hawk's left. Hawk hurried in that direction. Pushing a low-hanging bough out of his path, he crossed a moss-carpeted clearing and pushed into a thicket that bordered a further open patch.

Cautiously he looked around.

The pines were still. There was no wind sighing in their topmost branches. No birds sang. No tiny creatures scurried away. The whole world waited, it seemed. Then Hawk caught a flash of movement to his left. He spun in that direction and saw the erect, trembling tail of a chipmunk vanishing across a branch.

Hawk relaxed and was about to start across the clearing in front of him when behind him he heard a branch being rapidly brushed aside. He whirled. Rushing upon him like an enraged grizzly, Cahill bowled into Hawk. Hawk felt himself being thrown violently backward. His foot caught on an exposed root and he went down heavily under Cahill. He twisted away from the wounded man and was just in time to escape the deadly arc of Cahill's knife. Hawk had lost his Colt when he went down. Drawing the knife Tames Horses had given him, he sliced at Cahill's exposed shirtfront. The long, razor-sharp blade cut a neat swath across Cahill's belly, red blood surging instantly from the slash.

With a roar of pure fury, Cahill charged Hawk. Hawk slipped to one side, swiping at Cahill as the man lunged past, his blade this time tracing a neat red line across the man's chest. His eyes alight with pain and blood lust, Cahill lunged doggedly at Hawk, his apelike arm swinging viciously. Still on one knee, Hawk parried the thrust awkwardly. This time Cahill's blade sliced his left shoulder, drawing an instant stream of blood.

Encouraged, Cahill uttered a low growl and lunged at Hawk. Hawk stood his ground and met Cahill's charge, driving his blade deep into the man's groin. He felt the blade cutting through muscle until it came to bone. With a grunt of both pain and surprise, Cahill staggered back, looked down at his bloody torso, then turned and bolted like a three-legged beast back through the pines, Hawk close behind.

It was a bad move on Cahill's part. Before he could get any distance between himself and Hawk, he was forced to pull up on the edge of a steep drop. He whirled, crouching, to face Hawk. His appearance gave Hawk some comfort. Cahill's buckskin shirt hung from his frame, revealing a chest shiny with blood, and the gaping thigh wound was bleeding freely. The loss of blood already was affecting Cahill. His face was deathly pale, his eyes narrowed in pain and grim concentration.

Hawk slowed, then advanced cautiously.

"This is crazy, Cahill," Hawk told him reasonably. "You'll be a dead man if you don't take care of those wounds. Just tell me where I can find Bannister and that ship captain. Do that and I'll let you ride out of here."

"Nice of you, but I'm already done for, you bastard. So why should I tell you anything? Why should I help the man what killed me?"

"Damm it, Cahill, you're not dead yet. Where's Bannister?"

Cahill grinned. It was a terrible, white, sweaty grin that seemed to be coming at Hawk from the other side of the grave. "I'm on my way to hell, mister, and you're comin' with me!"

"No, Cahill! Where's Bannister? Is he in that warehouse below?"

Cahill's smile froze on his drawn face, and he charged. Hawk stood his ground and parried. Like two fencers with truncated swords, they thrust and wrestled, circled and dodged, their knives flicking out with the speed of snake's tongues. Soon, both men's clothes were hanging in bloody strips as each deadly flick of the other's knife found flesh to slice and muscle to rip. Scores of lacerations, each oozing blood, blossomed on their arms and torsos.

At last Cahill slumped to one knee, his face drawn and pale from loss of blood. Sensing his opportunity, Hawk rushed him. Cahill saw him coming and dropped hastily back . . . into space. Screaming, he toppled out of sight.

Hawk hurried to the edge and looked down. Ten feet below, Cahill had managed to grab hold of a juniper root. Below him was a sheer drop to the flat. Cahill was scrambling desperately to gain a foothold so he could pull himself up.

"Hang on," Hawk told him wearily.

Sheathing his knife, he started to ease himself over the edge, wondering why in hell he was bothering. A gasp, then a cry came from below. Glancing down, Hawk saw Cahill—too weak to hold on any longer—let go of the root and tumble almost straight down for ten or fifteen yards, strike a boulder embedded in the slope, then bounce loosely out into space to land at the foot of the slope, where he came to rest as still and lifeless as a discarded rag doll.

Hawk pulled himself back up onto the ledge and went to look for his Colt.

He caught sight of it in the deep grass where he had dropped it, and was bending to pick it up when he heard heavy feet approaching through the brush. Grabbing up the Colt, he spun about to see two men in front of him less then ten feet away, rifles on their hips, wolfish grins on their faces.

"You better drop that Colt," one of them advised.

It was good advice. Hawk dropped it.

He recognized both men. They were the same two he had discouraged when he caught them attempting to rape the two Nez Percé maidens. The one on the left was the one whose ear Hawk had mangled. The scar leading from his cheekbone was still fresh and quite visible. The other man was his lank, sandy-haired partner.

"Lookie what we got here, Lafe," said the one

with the torn ear. "Our old friend. The famous Golden Hawk."

The two men stepped closer until they were within a few feet of Hawk. Lafe picked up Hawk's Colt.

"We could blow a hole in his balls, right now, Pike," Lafe said, aiming the Colt at Hawk's crotch.

"Sure, we could," Pike agreed. "But, hell, Lafe, he wouldn't last more'n a few days with a hole down there. You know how that makes a man bleed."

Lafe leaned his horse face close to Hawk's. "He's right. You wouldn't last more'n a few days. And we sure do want you to last long, Mr. Hawk. Yessir, we surely do."

Pike kicked Hawk viciously in the groin. As Hawk spun to the ground and doubled up in pain, Pike stared down at him, grinning. Then he spat on him. "You'll see, Mr. Hawk. What we got in store for you will be a hell of a lot worse than death."

"Oh, don't worry. You'll die," Lafe assured him.

"But it'll take a while," Pike said, still grinning.

Lafe clubbed Hawk with the Walker Colt and Hawk's head exploded into darkness.

Hawk awakened with a blinding headache and the smell of salt strong in his nostrils. A chilling dampness clung to him, and he realized he was in the warehouse he had spotted earlier. His many knife wounds had begun to scab over, but he felt as if he had been rolled repeatedly in a briar patch. Every movement was painful. Gritting his teeth, he struggled to a sitting position.

His feet were manacled to a chain that ran under

cleats driven into the floorboards. All around him were unhappy Indians, some sitting with their backs against the wall, others huddled in miserable clusters alongside the rotting remnants of old horse stalls. Slops jars filled the place with a pervasive stench. Many of the Indians were chanting death songs over and over, others were simply moaning disconsolately. It was clear that for these Indians this incarceration was a kind of death in life.

Hawk was nearest the large double doors. Apparently, he had been the last one to be deposited in this huge shed. He put his hand to the crown of his head where he had been struck and felt a patch of scabbed blood covering the spot. The throbbing inside his skull caused him to squint as he looked about him. As he did so, he saw a familiar figure rise from one of the groups of Indians near the stalls and come toward him, carrying his chain.

Tames Horses.

His chain was just long enough to enable him to sit cross-legged beside Hawk. The Indian looked weary, but undaunted. There was a long, deep knife slash on the side of his face. Tames Horses' eyes glowed with pleasure and wonderment.

"How did Golden Hawk find Tames Horses?"

"I didn't," Hawk replied bluntly in the Nez Percé tongue. "I was following Pine Bluff's town marshal. He led me to this place. You mind telling me how in hell you showed up here too?"

Tames Horses shrugged. "Old Indian is like old buffalo. He like to feed on green grass. Mary Jane is fine woman."

"I don't doubt that. But you're not answering my question."

"We go swim in ocean. It is very cold. But we get used to it. We splash and play like crazy fish. Mary Jane laugh much. It is getting dark and her laugh, it go far, too far, I think."

"Go on."

"When it is dark, we wrap each other in blanket. While we get warm, shadows fall over us. I look up and see this man with the torn ear. He has friend with face of horse. They both have pistols."

"So you were taken by them."

He nodded unhappily. "This white man with torn ear, he say he hear Mary Jane's laugh. He come to investigate and say he watch us for long while. He say he can use me and Mary Jane. When I reach wagon, I find many Tillamook Indians inside. I try to take gun from Torn Ear's hand, but his friend stop me."

"That where you got the knife wound?"

The old Indian reached up to his cheek and nodded sheepishly.

"Where's Mary Jane?"

"She is below slope in small hut. Many Indian girls are with her. This captain will sell them all to rulers in China and India, maybe. I do not know these places."

"This captain, is his name Sutherland?"

"I not know his name. He is not come yet with his ship. When he comes, then we all go on long voyage in his great ship. We work very hard. This is what I hear."

"Who'd you hear it from?"

"A white man. He is asleep in corner."

"Bring him over."

"His chain cannot reach this far."

"How come yours is so long?"

"The one with the torn ear, he say I am big chief and let me have long chain so I can move about and help Indians who are sick. He think Tames Horses is old man and will not give him much trouble. He is fool."

"Did you see him bring me in?"

"Yes."

"When was that?"

"Yesterday."

"I've been out that long?"

"At first I think you dead. Your head bleed much. And you have many knife wounds. But then I hear your heart. It beat very loud and steady. So I let you sleep."

Hawk glanced up at the warehouse's loft and was just able to catch a glimpse of sky out of a window. Some light was filtering in through it, but not much. It would be dark soon. Reaching up, he found his captors had not discovered his throwing knife in its sheath at the back of his neck.

He withdrew it and handed it to Tames Horses. "Give this to the white man you mentioned. Help him use it to dig around the cleats holding his chain. When he's free bring him over here."

Tames Horses took the knife and dragged his chain toward a corner. Hawk watched him talking to the fellow propped up against the wall. Then Hawk reached out for the nearest slop jar and managed, despite his manacles, to use it. Feeling a whole hell of a lot better, he closed his eyes and gave in almost at once to the heavy exhaustion that still clung to his battered frame.

*   *   *

Tames Horses was shaking him gently. Hawk opened his eyes and sat up. Tames Horses and the white man were crouched beside him. The white man was a lean, weather-beaten fellow in his early thirties, with clear blue eyes, a square jaw, and sandy hair bleached almost white by the sun. He wore a band around his head to hold his thick hair in place and was dressed like a seaman, which he apparently was. He grinned at Hawk as he handed Hawk's knife back to him.

Hawk was aware that his head no longer pounded with the same fury as before. But he sure as hell was hungry.

"My name's Jed Thompson," he told the sandy-haired seaman.

"I'm Nat Carlson, Jed," the fellow replied, in an accent that revealed him for an easterner—an educated easterner, at that. "Many thanks for the use of that knife."

"It's just a start. We can use it to dig out the rest of these cleats. Then maybe we'll wrap this chain around someone's neck and get out of here."

"I appreciate those sentiments, Jed, but it took me and the chief four hours to dig out only one cleat. We'll be a week getting the rest free."

"Maybe."

"You mean you have some dynamite cached nearby—or more knives?"

"Trust me. Help me dig up my cleat and the two next to it. If we can get them free, we'll be able to hurry this business along."

"Sure, I'll lend a hand. But the thing is, all we have is that little throwing knife."

"It'll be sufficient. Besides, what choice do we have?"

"Can't argue with that," Carlson admitted.

Nat set to work on the cleat holding Hawk's chain. When he tired, Tames Horses took over. Then Hawk took his turn. Meanwhile, the rest of the Indians— there were close to a dozen chained together in the warehouse—rose to their feet and strained against their shackles to get a closer look at what the three men were doing. No longer were they chanting or moaning, and in their faces Hawk now saw a measure of hope.

With the three of them working steadily, the additional cleats were eventually pried loose. Hawk promptly got to his feet and took the chain in both hands.

"Carlson, you take hold of the chain," Hawk told him. "You too, Tames Horses."

"Now the thing is," explained Hawk, "it'll take the three of us pulling together under a full head of steam to budge the next cleat, and then the next. We might not be able to provide enough force, but I'm betting that if we can get a good-enough start, we can do it."

"Hell," said Nat, admiringly. "It makes good sense to me."

Hawk nodded. "When I give the signal, go."

Hawk made sure they were ready and had a good firm grip on the chain, then nodded. They rushed over the remaining cleats, running as hard as they could. The chain grew suddenly taut, strained for a moment at the cleat, then pulled it free. The three men marched back to their starting position and ran harder this time, managing to rip up two more cleats before one particularly tenacious bolt held. Again they backed up and repeated the process. The cleat was launched from the floorboard with such fury it rang off the wall like a horseshoe.

From that point on, it was only a matter of time. The longer the unencumbered chain grew and the greater the distance the men had for their run, the easier it became to rip up the remaining cleats. In less than a half-hour, the task was accomplished. Though they had no keys to unlock their individual shackles, at least now they could move about freely.

Then Hawk outlined his plan for breaking out. Using sign language mostly, Tames Horses relayed Hawk's scheme to the Indians. The basic plan was simplicity itself. All they had to do now was wait.

At daybreak, Hawk and Nat, peering through a narrow opening between two warped boards, saw a sailing ship approaching the cove. Hawk was impressed by its size and spread of sail. This was no mean merchantman, but a slim, graceful bird of the sea, similar to some of the finest clippers he had seen putting into Boston harbor. As he and Nat watched, Hawk saw seamen scrambling up its rigging to reef its canvas in preparation for sailing into the cove.

Nat said, "That's the *China Queen*, all right."

"A pretty ship."

"Maybe so. But her captain, Sutherland, is a cold-hearted bully, and his first mate is no better."

"You know this for a fact, do you?"

Nat laughed. "Hell's bells, Jed. Every port in

China and in the States knows that man and his reputation. Seamen who have served under him rounding the Cape know now that hell is a frigid, icebound place with a wind fit to peel off a man's skin."

Hawk chuckled at Nat's way of putting things. Ten years before, a Harvard graduate, he, along with all but one of his graduating class, had decided to make the sea their life's career. Seven were already masters of their own ships, and Nat himself had been first mate on the *Lightning*, a famous clipper ship that went down six months ago in a China Sea typhoon. It had been his additional misfortune to be taken on by a captain more reckless than wise, who had been unlucky enough to pile his ship onto rocks off the Alaskan coast.

Working his way south along the coast, heading for San Francisco and a shot at the goldfields, Nat stopped in at a tavern to wet his whistle. Unfortunately, it was a place run by a notorious crimp who doctored Nat's drinks. When Nat came to his senses, he was on his way to this cove, chained to the bed of a wagon along with six very unhappy Tillamook Indians, with Pike and Lafe in charge. These two were not gentle masters.

Hawk stepped away from the wall. The ship was here. Lafe and Pike would be arriving soon to drive their motley crew ahead of them down the steep bluff to the dock Hawk had glimpsed below, from there to be herded aboard the *China Queen*.

If nothing happened, that is, to stop them . . .

Hawk moved back to the spot where he had been left before and slumped down with his back to the wall after carefully fitting the cleat holding his section of chain into the holes that had held it. It had to appear to be still solidly embedded in the floor ... and still holding the chain in place. The Indians had long since been instructed in the necessity of this, and in a matter of a few moments everyone was sprawled on the floor, apparently safely chained up. Tames Horses had suggested that the Indians even commence their chants again in order to make the effect more convincing.

Surprise and speed were all they had to overcome their armed captors, and Hawk impressed this fact on every Indian. Or, more accurately, Tames Horses did.

The warehouse doors were suddenly swung wide. At once every head ducked away from the blinding light flooding in, every man seeming thoroughly cowed. With petty arrogance, Pike and Lafe strode into the warehouse at the head of four other seamen. All of them carried rifles and had pistols stuck in their belts. Lafe headed directly for Hawk and stopped in front of him.

"How's your head, Mr. Hawk?"

Hawk had no desire to precipitate anything at that moment. They could not make their move until every one of Lafe's men was so far inside the warehouse they would have no chance to escape back out when Hawk and the others attacked.

Hawk replied meekly, "My head still hurts, you bastard."

"You're lucky you still got one," Lafe replied, kicking Hawk viciously in the side.

Gasping, Hawk keeled over, careful not to yank

the chain against the loosened cleat. Enjoying the sight of Hawk's discomfort, Lafe stood over him awhile, then turned his back to him, planted his feet wide, and waved the rest of his men farther into the warehouse. One of the men held a large key, which opened the padlock holding the end of the chain to a cleat on the wall. Hawk assumed the men also had keys for the individual leg manacles.

The doors swung halfway shut as the men slowly moved farther into the place. Lafe watched them impatiently, waiting for the padlock to be unlocked so they could thread the chain back through the cleats and manacles. Hawk bent his head slightly until his eyes met those of Tames Horses and Nat. He nodded faintly.

At once Nat and Tames Horses jumped up—as did all the Indians in the warehouse—and rushed the six men, carrying their chains in their hands. Though they could not reach any great speed with their feet manacled, the element of surprise was such that they reached their captors and flung their long chains about them before a single one of them could cry out. As they went down under the brutal, killing lash of the chains, only a single shot rang out, and that was muffled by the Indian's body that took the slug.

The four seamen died cruelly but quickly. Pike managed to scramble to a corner and fight off his attackers for a minute or so, before being buried under a chain-wielding giant of an Indian.

On Hawk's orders, Lafe alone survived. Nat held him securely as Tames Horses hurried over to the doors and kept a lookout. Hawk planted himself in front of Lafe. The man was pale, trembling. He knew he was a dead man.

"Unlock these shackles, Lafe."

Lafe dropped to his knees and with trembling fingers inserted his key into the shackle's lock. Hawk stepped out of the manacles.

"Now take care of the others."

Kneeling obligingly before every man there, Lafe unlocked the cruel shackles that bound their ankles. When he was done, he looked over at Hawk, his eyes pleading. He had no pride. Where before he was the cruel taskmaster without a pinch of mercy, now he was a craven object of pity, trembling for his life.

Hawk preferred him the other way. He nodded to Nat, who in turn left Lafe to the Indians. Throttling his attempt to cry out, they dragged him off into a corner and took their time killing him.

They stood in front of the warehouse, staring down the sharp slope at the clipper ship sailing into the cove below—Hawk, Nat, Tames Horses, and one of the Tillamook, a tall, angular fellow with a fishbone in each earlobe. All four men were armed, as were eight other Tillamook Indians crouched behind them, some with rifles, some with pistols. They had wasted no time stripping the dead men of their firearms. Hawk had retrieved his Walker Colt and bone-handled knife from Lafe's body. And then, to his pleased surprise, he discovered that Pike had stripped Hawk's rifle from his dead horse and had been carrying it.

Now, as they watched, the clipper ship hove to and dropped anchor in the middle of the cove, the water near the shore evidently too shallow to allow the huge clipper to pull alongside the makeshift dock. Hawk noticed that the captain did not have much of a crew. He counted no more than six seamen on deck or clambering up the shrouds. No wonder Sutherland was desperate enough to shanghai Tillamook Indians.

"What next?" Nat asked Hawk.

"There's women somewhere below us in the cove. One in particular Tames Horses and I feel responsible for. We've got to free them before Sutherland and his crew reach shore."

Nat sighed. It was obvious he would have liked nothing better than to clear out immediately and get as far as possible from the clipper ship and its captain.

"Ain't you up to it, Nat?" Hawk asked.

"Remember, Jed. It's not just Sutherland's crew we got to worry about. The truth is we don't know how many men are down there guarding the women."

"That's right, Nat, we don't. But are you suggesting we leave those woman for Sutherland—so he can turn them over to some slave dealer to auction off to the highest bidder?"

Nat straightened and his jaw tightened with resolve. "Of course not."

"Didn't think so."

"I was just trying to remind you of the difficulties we're liable to encounter, that's all."

"Thanks. So maybe the best thing for us to do right now would be to slip down there and do some reconnoitering. See how many of Bannister's men there are down below before we make a move."

"Sounds prudent enough, I suppose."

"You don't sound too enthusiastic."

"I don't think enthusiasm has anything to do with it."

Hawk smiled. "Maybe you're right. Let's go."

Hawk told Tames Horses to keep the Indians inside the warehouse and out of sight until he and Nat returned. Tames Horses nodded in reply.

Hawk turned and followed Nat into some bushes, then down a well-worn path leading to the cove.

—8—

The path ended at a thick patch of timber that ran along the edge of the cove. They entered it, pushed on through it, and saw a two-story frame house and a horse barn sitting on a slight elevation at the other end of a long flat. Between the house and the barn was a stone-sided bunkhouse. From the house the cove was visible in its entirety.

Keeping to the woods, they came at the three buildings from the rear and then crept through the tall grass and bushes bordering the barn. From inside it came the restless stirring of horses in their stalls, the stomping of powerful feet.

They moved on past the barn to the bunkhouse and peeked into a window that opened onto a long room with heavy, massive beams in its ceiling. The room was occupied by the captured Indian women. There were at least ten of them. They were not chained or bound in any way and they reclined on their bunks, seemingly quite content with their lot. Quick, girlish laughter sounded often. Smiles brightened their dusky faces. Many were playing games on the blankets spread on their bunks, clapping hands often as they swept up the fallen bones or cast down the glass beads and polished stones, laughing delightedly at their sudden turns of fortune. Apparently they were looking forward to a life of sensual indolence in the harems of whichever Eastern potentates purchased them.

Hawk caught sight of Mary Jane. She was looking on from a distant bunk, leaning back against a corner. She was glowering unhappily at the Indian women about her, undoubtedly unable to understand a word of their language and at the same time finding their enthusiasm for this unexpected change in their lives incomprehensible. Which only meant that Mary Jane had never had to satisfy the imperious, sometimes brutal demands of an Indian husband. They weren't all as gentle and as mellow as Tames Horses.

Pulling away from the bunkhouse window, Hawk led Nat over to the rear of the two-story frame house. There was a small porch. Cautiously, they mounted it. Hawk drew his Walker and pulled open the back door, stuck his head into the kitchen, and finding it empty, listened intently. He heard the dim mutter of voices. Hawk entered the kitchen, Nat on his heels. Pausing again, Hawk heard distinctly now the sound of men's voices coming from the front of the house on the same floor.

Thumb-cocking his Colt, Hawk pushed through the kitchen door and moved on cat feet ahead of Nat down a narrow hallway, which brought him to a sliding double door leading to the living room. The doors were slid back halfway. Peering cautiously into the room, Hawk saw the backs of four armed men sitting around a table playing poker. A fifth man was at the front window. Like the others, he wore a wool cloth cap and, like tnem, had the unmistakable look and smell of a seaman. A knife and a pistol were stuck in his belt, and through a brass telescope he was studying the clipper ship riding at anchor in the cove.

Beside Hawk, Nat flattened against the wall. Hawk cursed himself for a fool. They had walked into a hornet's nest and were lucky there was no one above them on the stairs. Even so, one sound would bring the four men out of their chairs instantly.

The fellow at the window lowered his glass and addressed the four cardplayers over his shoulder. "The captain ain't lowered a boat yet."

"He'll take his time," one of the poker players said, studying his hand and then discarding two cards. "He's in no hurry. Not that one."

"Wait'll he sees what he's got for a crew," said the player beside him. As he spoke, he slapped down his cards and leaned back in his chair. There was a bottle sitting on the table. He took a swig from it.

"Hell, Sutherland ain't worried none about that," the man at the window replied, carefully focusing the telescope. "He says Indians make good sailors, once they learn to fear the belayin' pin."

"Only trouble is, you can't turn your back on 'em."

"No captain ever turns his back on a seaman," another player remarked. "Less'n he's prepared to kill the son of a bitch."

"Easy now," the player beside him remarked. "Them's harsh words for the likes of an able-bodied seaman."

"Maybe so. But it's the truth."

The poker player who had already folded clasped his hands behind his head. He was a little, wiry fellow with a round face and a knobby nose and quick, small brown eyes. "Well, now, as for this here tar," he told the others, "he ain't never goin' to feel a deck heave beneath his feet again. He's a landlubber for good now. You might say he's done lost his sea legs."

"Hell's fire, Dinty," said the dealer, glancing shrewdly at him. "You lost your sea legs in bed with all them Indian squaws out there."

"No sense in denying it," Dinty said, sighing contentedly. "Just don't tell Bannister, that's all. He's a real nut when it comes to delivering what he calls virgins."

"Yeah. Him and that captain."

The game proceeded without further comment as the dealer dealt each player staying in the cards requested. Accepting the new cards, the players studied their hands and began betting. It was brisk, and real gold coin was being shoved into the pot. Two of them stayed throughout the bidding as the dealer and another player discarded their hands. The winner displayed a full house, king high, and as he swept his winnings toward him, the deal was passed to the next man.

Hawk had already cocked his Walker, so that sound would not betray his presence if he decided to step into the room and jump the five men. But Nat would have to move as fast as Hawk and not gum things up. In addition, Hawk did not know for sure who might be upstairs. Or who might be outside in the barn, ready to run into the place if gunfire erupted. Any miscalculation on Hawk's part and this living room could turn into a mean killing ground.

Hawk turned his head to look at Nat. What he saw convinced him not to make any foolish moves. Nat's face was sheet-white. Beads of cold sweat stood out on his forehead. He was obviously close to panic.

With a smile designed to calm Nat down, Hawk jerked his head, indicating Nat should back up so they could return to the kitchen. Nat nodded eagerly and moved cautiously backward down the hallway. It was strange. They had left the kitchen and moved down this passage with relative ease, not making a sound, but as they neared the kitchen, it seemed that every board underfoot protested loudly.

"Someone out there?" one of the men called suddenly.

Ducking into the kitchen, Hawk and Nat froze beside the doorway. Someone got up from his chair and strode into the hallway and stood there, evidently gazing down the empty passage into the kitchen.

"Hey! Come on back, Mike. I want to play out this hand."

"Thought I heard something."

It seemed like a very long time before Hawk heard the man's footsteps retreating into the living room. A moment later the chatter about the table picked up again.

"Now that I think of it, where's Pike and the others?" a player asked, revealing some annoyance.

"Yeah," another replied. "They should've brought them redskins down here by now."

"You want me to go up there and check on 'em?" asked one of them. Hawk recognized the voice as belonging to the little one they called Dinty.

"Finish the game first."

Hawk and Nat stole out of the kitchen, letting the back door close softly behind them. They jumped to the ground and flattened themselves against the outside wall.

"What now?" asked Nate. "There's five of them and only two of us."

"We could have taken them."

"I was in favor of that, but I didn't know if you were."

"You ever handled a gun before, Nat?"

"No."

"That's what I thought."

"All I have to do is pull the trigger. Right?"

"There's more to it than that."

Nat swallowed unhappily. "I know it," he said. "I admit it. As a matter of fact, I'm a liar. I'm glad we didn't try anything."

"So am I. We'd better go back up for Tames Horses and the others. With them Indians, it'll be over in no time."

"We better hurry. One of 'em's coming up to check on the delay."

"And when he does, we'll be waiting."

"What about the captain and his crew?"

"One thing at a time, Nat."

Without further discussion, the two hurried back into the timber and up the bluff. Tames Horses was sitting cross-legged in front of the warehouse's open doors. He was alone. The warehouse behind him was empty. The Tillamook Indians were gone, every damned one of them.

"My red brothers did not wait," Tames Horses said glumly.

"I should have thought of that," sighed Hawk.

"I tell them to stay and free their women," Tames Horses explained. "But they not listen. They are not brave warriors, like the Nez Percé and other horse Indians."

Hawk suggested they get out of sight. They were expecting a visitor from below soon, and the hope was they could take him quietly, if at all possible.

They did not have to wait long for their visitor.

As Hawk had expected, he was the one they called Dinty, the fellow who had lost his sea legs. As he toiled up the path, his pistol stuck in his belt, he didn't appear to suspect anything.

Crouching in the bushes at the head of the path, Hawk let Dinty move on past him. Tames Horses was waiting inside the warehouse, Hawk's rifle in his hand. A still-nervous Harvard graduate was on the other side of the path holding a pistol he was hoping he would not have to use.

The seaman came to an abrupt halt at the edge of the grassy flat leading to the warehouse. Frowning, he craned his head to get a better look at the warehouse doors. He could see they were no longer tightly shut. Furthermore the warehouse was quiet, too damned quiet. There should have been the sound of unhappy, chanting Indians coming from within it.

"Hey! Pike Simms," he called nervously. "Lafe? You in there?"

There was no response. Dinty loosened the pistol in his belt and continued on to the warehouse, this time much more cautiously. Hawk left the bushes, ran up lightly behind him, and tapped him on the shoulder. The seaman whirled around. Hawk caught him on the point of his jaw with the barrel of his Colt. The little seaman went down without a sound.

Tames Horses came out of the warehouse and dragged the man inside, locking him into a set of manacles. Then he left the place and closed the warehouse doors.

"Only four more to go," Hawk told the Indian.

Nat came up beside them. He seemed very relieved. "Much better odds," he said.

Hawk led the way back down the path.

A few moments later, as they reached the edge of the timber shielding the buildings, a shot rang out from the brush near the house. A round nipped a branch just over Hawk's head. Hawk ducked low. So did Nat and Tames Horses. Stealth, it seemed, was no longer an option. The rest of Bannister's men had discovered them.

Beside him Tames Horses frowned unhappily. "Damn fish Indians," he said. "We set them free, then they go and leave us."

"We don't need them," Hawk said. "Spread out. We'll surround the bastards."

Nat looked at him. "What do you mean?"

"You still got that pistol?"

Nat nodded.

"When you get close enough to one of them seamen, use it. We'll take them out one at a time. But we better hurry. That shot is going to bring the captain and his crew ashore pretty damn quick."

Tames Horses tapped Nat on his shoulder and beckoned to him. Relieved to have a companion, Nat slipped off through the trees with him, while Hawk moved straight ahead, his eye on a corner of the house. A second before, he had caught there the quick gleam of sunlight on metal.

He kept in cover until the last possible moment, then raced out of the woods, heading for the back corner of the house. It was the dealer who stepped into view and flung up his rifle. Hawk lunged to one side, landed on his belly, rolled over twice, then came up firing. Two rounds slammed into the man, knocking him back. Hawk kept on coming.

From a second-story window another shot came. Hawk felt the round whisper past his cheek. Then he was behind the house. The man he shot was flat on his back, his eyes open wide. He was not breathing.

Darting past him, Hawk stormed into the kitchen, raced down the hallway, and bolted up the stairwell. A shot from the room at the head of the stairs took out a balustrade behind him, and Hawk ducked facedown onto the stairs.

He was in a bad spot. But at least the son of a bitch in the room was not going anywhere. Slowly, cautiously, he lifted his head. Another shot took out part of the stair tread inches from his forehead. Tiny shards of wood bit into his face. He ducked low again, thumb-cocked, braced himself, then launched himself up the stairs, firing into the room as he came.

There was no answering fire from inside the room.

Hawk flattened himself against the wall beside the open door and waited, listening. He heard nothing. Whoever was in there was probably busy reloading his pistol.

Suddenly, a plaintive voice came from the room. "Who the hell are you, mister? What's this all about?"

Hawk recognized the voice of the poker player who had had the full house. He sounded as if he knew his luck had changed.

"You mean you don't know who I am?"

"Lafe and Pike mentioned you, I think. Said you was called Hawk, or something. Said you was after Bannister. It sounded crazy. You comin' this far."

"Maybe it's crazy, but I'm here. Toss your gun out and maybe we can talk."

"How can I trust you?"

"You don't have much choice, mister. I didn't come alone."

There was a moment of silence as the fellow thought over his position. Then he threw out his gun. It bounced on the wooden floor and spun to a halt at Hawk's feet. Hawk picked it up and stuck it in his belt.

"All right," Hawk said. "Come out of there . . . slowly."

The man appeared in the room's doorway, then paused uncertainly, watching Hawk warily.

Hawk waggled his gun at the man. "Come on," he urged. "We ain't got all day."

The man strode out onto the landing. "What do you want to know?"

"I want Bannister. Where is he?"

"He ain't here."

"I know that, damm it. Is he on that ship?"

"No. He gets too sick when's he's on a boat—a clipper ship, especially. He wouldn't be on it."

"Where's it coming from?"

"San Francisco."

"What about the girl Bannister took?"

"You mean that blonde?"

"That's right."

"I don't know nothin' about her. Bannister just hired me to bring in them Indians up there until Sutherland got back."

"You didn't do a very good job."

"It's a lousy job. If I get out of this, I'll never crimp another damned redskin—not for the rest of my life."

"Maybe you mean that."

"I do, so help me."

From outside the house came a shot and a scream, then silence. A moment later there was another single shot. Then silence again. Hawk glanced at the man in front of him. Aside from this fellow, there was only one man left, assuming Nat and Tames Horses had done their jobs.

The seaman shifted unhappily, his eyes on the gun in Hawk's hand. "What's going on, mister?"

"I got a small army out there, cleaning up your mates. But you'll be all right. Just tell me where I can find Bannister."

The fellow moistened his dry lips. "Up the coast, there's a cove—"

From the floor below came running feet. The seaman turned his head to look down the stairwell. A sudden blast of gunfire came from the foot of the stairs. The seaman buckled as the slugs from below ripped into him. There was a startled look on his face. His eyes caught Hawk's for an instant. It seemed as if the man were crying.

Then he toppled headfirst down the stairs. Hawk strode to the edge of the landing. The fifth sailor, a smoking rifle in his hands, was staring at his friend tumbling down the staircase toward him.

"Hold it right there," Hawk demanded.

The fellow was too much of a fool. Dropping his empty rifle, he snatched a pistol from his belt and hauled it up. Before he could fire, Hawk sent a round into his chest, then thumb-cocked and sent a second round after the first. The man crushed backward and came to rest on the floor, his back hard against a wall. A puddle of blood slowly spread under him.

As he hurried down the stairs, Hawk reloaded his Colt. Reaching the living room, he glanced out the front window. Nat and Tames Horses were hurrying toward the house. He stepped over to the front door and flung it open.

"What happened, Nat? Get your feet wet?"

Nat nodded unhappily.

Tames Horses smiled slightly as he glanced at Nat. "He use gun, but he hit stomach, let sailor scream."

"Couldn't help it," said Nat. "But he's dead enough. Another one came at me and Tames Horses saved my life with his shot."

Tames Horses confirmed, "Both men dead."

"Then all five are accounted for," Hawk noted.

"We better hurry anyway," Nat said. "I saw crewmen putting out from the ship. One of them was the captain."

"How many?"

"Six, not counting the captain."

"Enough to be a real headache," Hawk admitted.

"What about Mary Jane?" Tames Horses asked. "Where is she?"

"Follow me," Hawk told him.

Entering the bunkhouse, they found the women huddled on their cots, frightened. They had heard the gunfire, and most of them were terrified that they were going to be released and have to go back to their people.

But when Mary Jane saw them, she cried out, raced down the room, and hurled herself into Hawk's arms. "I knew you'd come," she whooped.

Tames Horses nodded solemnly. "You all right?"

"Hey, Chief," she cried, hugging him too. "I'm just fine. Now let's get the hell out of here."

"What about them?" Nat asked, indicating the Indian women.

"Leave 'em be," Hawk said. "They're goin' to be mighty unhappy when they find out they ain't goin' on a sea voyage."

"And we better see about the captain and that boat full of seamen."

They left the bunkhouse and made for the edge of the cove. Screened by bushes, they peered out at the lifeboat. It was no longer heading for the dock. The rowers had shipped their oars, and the boat was bobbing on the water a good distance from the pier.

The captain stood up.

"Ahoy, there! What's afoot?"

Disguising his voice as best he could, Hawk called

out, "Come ahead, Captain. We had some trouble, is all."

"What kind of trouble?"

"Hurry up," Hawk called back, his voice effectively muffled. "We'll be needin' some help!"

This appeared to satisfy the captain. He sat back down. The seamen lowered their oars into the water and began pulling for the dock.

"We'll be down there, waiting for them," said Hawk, grinning.

A cry echoed across the cove, followed by the sound of a splash. Looking back through the bushes, Hawk saw someone swimming hard for shore. He had just dived off the clipper ship and was heading directly toward them. Hawk could not be sure, but from the bright gleam of his sun-bleached hair, it looked like he had found young Sam Baldwin.

At once the rowboat reversed in an effort to intercept the swimmer. The captain, crouching in the bow of the rowboat, began firing at him. Geysers of water spouted about Sam's head.

"Damn!" cried Hawk.

He snatched his rifle from Tames Horses, lifted it to his shoulder, and fired on the captain. The round missed the captain, but one of his sailors dropped his oar and pitched forward into the boat. Thoroughly alerted now, the captain ducked low and shouted to his men to row back to the ship. Hawk ran out from behind the bushes, reloading quickly, lifted the Hawken to his shoulder, and sent a second round after the captain. He could not be sure, but he thought this time he might have hit him.

But it made no difference, Hawk thought bitterly as he lowered his rifle. The captain would make it back to his ship and weigh anchor. They had lost any chance they might have had to capture him and his crew and take over the ship.

Below him a sputtering, exhausted Sam Baldwin staggered through the surf, collapsing finally on the sand.

"Who's that up there?" he called feebly, looking up at Hawk.

"Don't you recognize me, lad?"

"You!"

"That's right. The same man you cut loose in that wagon. I've been looking for you and your sister."

The boy tried to rise, but couldn't quite manage it. He was more than done in; he was close to collapse. Hawk, Nat, and Tames Horses scrambled down the steep embankment to the beach. Nat flung the boy over his shoulder and carried him back up the slope and into the house. As soon as Nat laid Sam down on the sofa, Mary Jane bent over him anxiously, then asked someone to bring a glass of water. As Nat went for it, Hawk heard a commotion outside and hurried out onto the front porch. Tames Horses joined him.

A disconsolate band of Tillamook Indian women, waving and calling to the ship, were running across the meadow in front of the house, heading for the dock. In a moment they had reached it and were streaming out onto it, waving and calling even more frantically.

But no one on the ship paid them the slightest

heed as the crewmen and the captain clambered up the ship's side. The lifeboat was hauled quickly aboard, and with commendable speed the ship weighed anchor and came about. Unfurling its sails, it heeled out of the cove and headed north, leaving behind a dock full of unhappy Indian women.

But they were not abandoned for long. Out of the trees behind the dock suddenly swarmed the shang-haiied Tillamook braves. As they crowded onto the dock, their women greeted them with shrill cries of outrage and bitter, futile anger. It was a wild scene, but after a short, furious scuffle, the women of the Tillamook tribe were brought under control by their menfolk and hauled off to resume their lives as dutiful wives and mothers.

Chuckling, Hawk went back inside the house.

Sam was sitting up on the sofa, sipping a mug of coffee. Mary Jane had found the coffeepot and the bracing smell of freshly made brew filled the house.

"What were you doing on that ship, Sam?"

"You might say I was lucky."

"What the hell do you mean by that?"

"Captain Sutherland and his first mate are wild men. Any seaman that doesn't jump to their orders gets beaten raw. After Bannister's men handed me over to Sutherland, I saw two men thrown overboard on the run up the coast. They were beaten so bad, you couldn't even recognize them."

"No wonder he has to use crimps to get a crew," Nat remarked.

"So how were you lucky?" Hawk asked.

"I didn't have to climb the rigging or do any work aloft. The captain made me his cabin boy. He was hoping Marta would take the voyage better if I was on board."

"Where is she now?"

"I don't know," Sam said miserably.

"What do you mean, you don't know?"

"She's still with Bannister and that shipment of furs he took from the fort. The captain was on his way to meet him when he stopped in here for the crew Bannister promised him."

"Where was the captain supposed to meet Bannister?"

"A cove, somewhere along the coast north of here."

"Where, dammit? We've got to reach the spot before he gets there."

"Mr. Thompson, I don't know where it is. It could be anywhere along the coast."

"Leave the boy alone," Mary Jane said, hurrying in from the kitchen. "I got some eggs on. I don't know about you, but I'm starved."

Hawk took a deep breath and remembered how hungry he was. Not a man protested the sudden meal. Every man there had a gaping hole for a stomach. With a weary sigh, Sam lay back down on the sofa.

Hawk went back outside onto the front porch and stared out at the ocean, Tames Horses and Nat by his side. Slumping down on the porch steps, Hawk shook his head. He found himself recalling what old Elias Smithers had tried to tell him. If the old geezer hadn't had such a sieve for a memory, maybe they would know now where to find Bannister.

Hawk turned to Nat. "You know many of the likely anchorages north of here?"

"There's plenty, Jed. All up and down the coast."

"Every hear of a Book Tavern?"

Nat frowned and tipped his head. "Now, wait a minute. Say that again, will you?"

"You heard me. Book Tavern. An old Quaker Bannister captured back there in the mountains said he heard Bannister mention Book Tavern."

Nat's eye lit. "Jed, he didn't mean Book, he meant hook. Hook Tavern."

"Hook Tavern? You mean you know such a place?"

"Hell, Jed," Nat cried. "That's where I was given that drugged drink. Hook Tavern is run by crimps."

"Where is it?"

"North of here near a small village. Place called Bay City."

Hawk remembered something else old Elias had heard Bannister mention. It had sounded like rove to Elias. What Elias *could* have heard was cove. "Nat, is the tavern near a harbor—or a cove."

"Sure. There's a cove less than a mile north of it."

"What's it called?"

Nat thought a minute. "I don't rightly know if it has a name. It's a long winding cove with plenty of protection from the wind."

"Would you say it curves back on itself?"

"Yeah. I would."

"Like a hook, maybe," Hawk suggested.

"Damn, Jed! You're right! Like a giant fishhook."

Both men turned to Tames Horses, grinning at him like idiot children.

"What is matter with you two?" Tames Horses demanded.

"I think we better go find out what kind of horse-flesh we got in that barn," Hawk told him. "We're going to be riding north, looks like. We got a ship to catch."

"You find Bannister?"

"Maybe. Now let's go look over them horses."

Tames Horses nodded and descended the steps, heading for the horse barn, Hawk following after. Behind them, Nat pushed into the house to tell Sam the good news.

—9—

Hawk entered Hook Tavern carrying no visible weapons. His rifle, knife, and Walker Colt had been cached back where the five of them had left their horses—in a thick stand of Douglas fir on the ridge overlooking Hook Cove. He was alone and wanted it that way.

The small, smoke-filled tavern was crammed with sailors, farmers, teamsters. The local Indians were crowded in one corner away from the whites, dressed in fantastic combinations of white and Indian attire. They wore bowler hats, beaver hats, wide-brimmed felt hats, and all had stuck in them feathers of various size and shapes. Those few who wore pants had cut the crotches and butts out of them and replaced them with breechclouts. They were gloriously, foolishly drunk.

The bar itself was a long, unpretentious slab of wood supported by four wooden barrels and finished off with a varnished slab of Douglas fir. Hawk slouched over to the bar, keeping the brim of his hat down over his forehead, asked for a bottle and a mug, paid up, then found a table in a corner.

It was late. Very late. They had ridden full-tilt through the day and into the night, changing mounts often, and had reached Hook Cove before the clipper ship. Hawk was genuinely exhausted, but it was his task now to inveigle the unsuspecting barkeep into crimping him—and bringing him face to face with Bannister.

He had no intention of swallowing the foul concoction of rum and water contained in the bottle he had purchased. Partially hidden in the shadows of the corner table, he spat out the rum he drank against the already damp wall beside his chair. In this manner he finished the bottle, then returned to the bar for another. He was careful to make his progress through the crowd to the bar appropriately unsteady, shoving aside a few burly teamsters on the way. His voice was loud when he ordered, his speech slurred. The performance was impeccable. When he caught the conspiratorial gleam in the barkeep's eye, he knew he had convinced the man that in Hawk he had found an apprentice seaman for the long passage to the Orient.

Hawk returned to his table and managed to get rid of most of the bottle's contents by slopping it over the edge of the table as he poured the rum into his mug. He sat up to look around the room and saw that no one in particular had noticed him, but that the clientele was thinning out. Even some of the Indians, clinging to one another, were reeling out the tavern's door.

A beer mug shattered to bits against the wall inches above his head.

Hawk put his mug down carefully and turned to look full into the face of the teamster who had thrown it. He was a giant of a man with a gray beard and long, silvery hair that hung in thick, unkempt curls down onto his shoulders. A necklace of bear claws hung about his neck. If it was there for luck, it hadn't given him much, judging from his appearance. One wild, red-rimmed eye squinted permanently, the result of a fearsome wound that had torn off most of his eyelid. A long, ugly scar ran the length of his forehead, giving him a perpetual frown. As the big fellow moved closer to Hawk's table, he straightened his shoulders threateningly in preparation for the upcoming battle.

Under any other circumstances, Hawk would not have minded a fight. But this business could well throw a monkey wrench into his plans. He poured himself another drink. Before he could lift the mug to his lips, however, a bottle shattered against the wall inches from his face, splattering him with bad whiskey.

"What's the trouble, Graybeard?" Hawk asked, smiling pleasantly. "You got me mistaken for someone else, have you?"

"I ain't mistaken, you goddamn son of a bitch."

"I see. You just don't like me."

"You stepped on my foot back there. That ain't polite. Besides, I don't like the way you smell."

"I see. Well, as a matter of fact, I don't like the way I smell, either. Is there a good barber hereabouts where a man can get himself a bath?"

"Sure. The ocean's right outside." The tavern was as silent as a tomb through all this. The teamster smiled happily about him at the onlookers. "Anyone want to help me give this shitface a dip in the drink?"

No one stepped forward, which was a relief to Hawk.

"Forget it, friend," he said to Graybeard. "Go on back to your mates. I got some heavy drinking to do."

With that the teamster reached back to the bar for another beer mug and sent it hurtling at Hawk. It shattered against the wall. Had Hawk not ducked, the heavy mug would have smashed his skull. Hawk saw then that there was no way out of this—that everyone left in the place was watching with eager, glittering eyes. This was evidently a show they had been treated to often by the teamster. It was part of the night's entertainment, and this night it was Hawk's turn.

Hawk glanced quickly over at the barkeep. He was watching intently, aware of how much rum Hawk had consumed. Though a few minutes before Hawk had portrayed a man half out on his feet, he would now have to reveal how little effect the drugged liquor had actually had on him. He was in trouble, it seemed, no matter what he did.

But first things first.

He got quickly to his feet, swaying deliberately to entice Graybeard into a false sense of security. The big man responded on cue. Grinning like a possum eating yellow jackets, he strode swiftly toward Hawk. When he was close enough, Hawk snatched up a chair and broke it over Graybeard's head. It staggered him momentarily. But he shook it off and lurched heavily for Hawk, his big, branchlike arms stretched out. His method, apparently, was to force combat as he just had, then hug his opponents to death, or until he had cracked enough of their ribs to cause them to cry uncle.

Hawk ducked low and, driving straight ahead, slammed his right shoulder into Graybeard's midsection, pushing him violently back. The big fellow tripped over a chair and went crashing down on top of it, reducing it to kindling.

Hawk picked up a chair rung and bounced it off the teamster's head. It rang like a gong, but had little effect on the man, who twisted the rung out of Hawk's hand and flung it aside. Hawk jumped off the man, then kicked him in the side of the head. It caused Graybeard's eyes to blink, but had no other apparent effect.

Breathing heavily, Hawk glanced over again at the bartender. He was watching all of this carefully, but was apparently in no hurry to bring the contest to a halt.

Graybeard was bent over like a bear, his eyes blinking at Hawk, gathering himself to charge. Hawk waited. Graybeard lunged forward, coming fast. Hawk stood his ground. At the last possible moment, he skipped aside, grabbed the back of Graybeard's shirt collar, and running alongside him, slammed him headfirst into the wall. The wall did not budge an inch, but there was a sickening crunch as the top of Graybeard's skull broke like the shell of a hard-boiled egg. Hawk let Graybeard's bulk slam to the floor. The big man struck facedown, then sagged over onto his side. Blood seeped out from under his disheveled gray locks. His eyes were wide, startled, unblinking.

He had put on his last show for Hook Tavern's patrons.

Hawk heard a heavy tread behind him. Before he could turn completely, a belaying pin crunched down on the back of his neck. His knees turned to water and he tumbled headforemost into oblivion.

Hawk opened his eyes. It was night. The only light was coming from the moon's dim rays filtering in through a round porthole behind him. Nat was bent close to him, shaking him by the shoulders. Hawk had some difficulty at first focusing his eyes and sensed that Nat had been shaking him for a good long time.

"Okay, I'm coming around," Hawk managed. "Ease up, Nat."

The look of desperation on Nat's face faded. Sighing with relief, Nat leaned back, but remained crouched beside Hawk's low bunk.

Hawk could feel the ship rocking under him, its beams creaking. Sitting up on his elbows, he looked about him at the other bunks and saw strange and foreign faces peering at him curiously. He stared back at them with just as much curiosity.

Hawk smiled wanly at Nat. "Looks like I made it on board, all right."

"Yep. You were delivered less than two hours ago. They slipped a rope through your armpits and hauled you up like a big, dead fish. You didn't look all that good when you hit the deck. I thought you weren't going to drink any of that rum they serve in that place."

"I didn't. That wasn't what did me in. While I was busy fighting off a crazy teamster, I got hit from behind."

"You mean you tangled with that feller, the teamster built like a grizzly?"

Hawk nodded. "He didn't give me much choice."

"I saw him when I stopped there. Everyone steered clear of him if they could. I learned the crimps use him when they run out of dope for the drinks. He picks a fight, and before long it's all over."

"You mean that was his job? The crimps paid him to do that?"

"That's what I heard."

"Well, he won't be crimping anymore."

"Why not?"

"He's dead."

"Jesus! That man was indestructible. He'd take on all comers and never lose."

"I didn't mean to kill him. But like I said, he didn't give me much of a choice." Hawk reached back and rubbed his sore neck, then sat up. "How did you get on board?"

"Sam and I came with the furs. It took six trips in two longboats to haul them hides out to the ship. We hid among the plews. We slipped into the water when we reached the ship and waited for a chance to climb aboard."

"Where are the others?"

"Tames Horses and Mary Jane are still ashore. Right now, Sam's prowling the ship, looking for his sister."

"She's already aboard?"

"Bannister brought her on board as soon as the furs were stowed. And it looks like he's staying on with her."

Hawk shook his sore head and squinted about him. "Looks like I didn't need to get myself flattened, after all."

"Oh, yes, you did."

"All you had to do was watch the cove."

"We're not at Hook Cove. That crimp led us to another cove where Sutherland had anchored. Otherwise, we'd be waiting for the *China Queen* yet."

Hawk shook his head, bemused. Their luck was holding. He swung his legs down off the bunk and stood up. Nat stood up also and looked about at the sullen faces. From the look of them, this watch was little more than a baleful gang of cutthroats."

"You think these crewmen down here might throw in with us? There's no doubt they hate the captain, the first mate, especially."

"We better wait. Let them see which way the wind is blowing. Otherwise, they might only get in our way."

They moved up the stairs through the hatch to the upper deck. They were heading for the quarter deck when Sam appeared, hurrying to intercept them. He looked distraught.

"Did you find Marta?" Hawk asked.

"I found her," the boy answered miserably.

"What's wrong? Has Bannister hurt her?"

"It's not Bannister. It's Marta. She wants to stay with him."

"With Bannister?"

His lips compressed in shame and bitterness, Sam nodded. Nat looked at Hawk. "Looks like you came a long ways for nothing."

"Maybe so. But we got Sam here, and I want to hear this from Marta herself."

Nat shrugged. "Then let's get on with it."

Hawk turned to Sam. "Show us to Bannister's cabin."

They were nearing Bannister's cabin belowdecks

when the first mate and two crewmen stepped out into their path.

"What are you two doing here?" the first mate demanded of Hawk and Nat, assuming they were recent additions to the ship's crew. Then he glanced at Sam. "Back, are you, Sam? I thought you jumped ship."

"Leave us be, Blacky," said Sam. "We've come for my sister."

"Have you now?"

Blacky was a solidly built, dark-haired fellow with bushy eyebrows and smoldering blue eyes. He looked like a storm coming over a horizon, and from the many scar ridges on his face, it was clear he did not mind mixing it up. He was holding a marlin spike in his right hand and there was a wild eagerness for battle on his face. The two seamen with him, however, did not seem to share his enthusiasm for battle. As Blacky advanced on Hawk and Nat, they slunk back out of the way.

"You're a dead man, Blacky," said Hawk. "Stand fast now."

Blacky flipped the marlin spike and grinned—and kept on coming.

"I'm warning you," Hawk told him.

Blacky laughed contemptuously. "I'm going to wrap this marlin spike around your head, mister. If you're going to serve on this ship, you better learn to take orders."

Hawk reached back for his throwing knife and sent it through the air. It sank into the hollow of Blacky's throat. He yanked the small blade out and flung it to the deck. Then, uttering a gurgling sound, he sank to his knees.

Hawk glanced over at the two seamen to see what their intentions were. They turned tail and ran.

Hawk retrieved his knife, wiped it, and sheathed it. He turned to Sam. The boy was looking with pure horror at Blacky, who was lying on his side on the deck, both hands clasping his neck in a desperate, futile effort to stem the flow of blood. Because of the injury to his vocal cords, the first mate was unable to cry out.

"Keep going, lad," Hawk told him. "No time now for fainthearts."

Sam looked at Hawk, uncomprehending. Then he blinked and shook himself out of it. "This way," he said. "Down this passage."

When they came to the cabin door, Sam paused and stepped aside. Hawk pushed the door open and stepped inside the cabin, Sam and Nat following. Resplendent in a silk, ruby-red robe, Bannister was standing in the center of the cabin. On the silken coverlet of a large, canopied bed—an amazing extravagance for a clipper ship—Marta was reclining, wearing a gown so transparent it hid absolutely nothing. Pulling up, Hawk frowned. The close air in the cabin had a sickly sweet, cloying smell.

Bannister reached into the pocket of his robe and pulled out a small pistol. He leveled it at the three of them.

"Stand back," he told them.

Hawk stayed where he was, as did Nat and Sam.

"You've come a long way, Hawk," Bannister said. "I been expecting you. Until Sam's visit a while ago, I'd hoped my men had taken care of you. I see now I should have handled the matter myself."

His eyes were glassy, fogged. He raised the pistol.

"Don't shoot him, Martin," Marta cried. "You mustn't!"

"Why not, my dear?"

"Let him go. Please! And Sam, too. They don't understand."

"What is there to understand, Marta?" Hawk asked, stepping closer. "That Bannister has made you an addict? That you'll stay with him only because he feeds the habit he forced on you?"

Her eyes widened in surprise that Hawk should know so much. Then her face paled and she dropped her eyes, shamed, defeated. "Yes," she admitted softly, her voice hushed, barely audible. "If you must know. Yes."

Bannister swung about to face Marta. "But, Marta! That's not the only reason you're staying with me. Admit it. You love me!"

"Do you really believe that, Martin?" she spat bitterly. "My God! How could you not know. I stay with you only because you supply what I must have. I'm the slave of that vile pipe you fix for me every night—just as you are!"

Hawk moved swiftly. Before Bannister could duck away, Hawk was at his side, twisting the pistol from his grasp. It was a simple matter. In fact, Bannister seemed as insubstantial as a hollow reed, an emaciated counterfeit of the man Hawk had faced in the mountains.

Hawk glanced at the dresser. Sitting on top of it were two recently filled opium pipes waiting only for the match. In dealing with the Orient, Bannister had acquired one of its most fatal and debilitating vices.

"Where were you planning on taking her, Bannister?" Hawk asked. "To the land of the lotus-eaters?"

"What do you know of such things?" Bannister asked contemptuously.

"It doesn't matter, Bannister. You're coming with me. You have a lot to answer for."

"What are you men doing in here?!"

This loud, angry query came from behind Hawk. He turned about to see a man who was obviously Captain Sutherland stepping into the cabin, a pistol in his hand. When he saw young Sam with Hawk, he frowned, but did not lower his pistol.

Behind him, two crewmen stepped silently and swiftly into the cabin. Before Bannister could warn the captain, one of the crewmen dropped his arm over Sutherland's head and tightened it against his windpipe. Dropping his gun, the captain struggled desperately, futilely, to free himself.

Hawk hurried over, picked up the captain's gun, then shook the two crewmen off Sutherland. The captain reeled back against a bulkhead, clutching at his neck as he sucked deep gutfulls of air into his lungs.

"The first mate's dead," Hawk told the two crewmen. "You don't have to serve on this ship any more. You can abandon it if you want. Tell the other crewmen."

With a whoop, the crewmen turned and dashed out of the cabin to spread the word.

Hawk looked back at Sutherland. His face had regained its color. It was dark now with rage. "Without a crew," Hawk reminded him, "you'll be helpless, Captain."

"Not every crewman will abandon me."

"Then you've got nothing to worry about, have you, captain," said Nat, grinning. "Bon voyage!"

"Damn you men! This is my ship! Get off it!"

"Sure. We'll do that," Hawk told him. "But we're taking this girl and Bannister with us."

"Then take them. Take them both. Do you think I care? The woman is of no use to anyone. Her will is sapped completely. And Bannister's addiction has destroyed whatever value he might have once possessed."

Hawk turned back to Marta and Bannister. There was nothing either exotic or exciting about either of them now, despite Bannister's ruby red robe or the canopied bed upon which Marta reclined in her translucent nightgown. They looked now like unhappy children caught behind a barn, their faces drawn, the thin pale light of defeat in their eyes.

"Get dressed, both of you," Hawk told them sharply. "We'll be waiting for you on deck. And hurry it up, or we'll be back for you."

Hawk then waggled the pistol at the captain, who turned and preceeded him from the cabin.

Topside, the crew was leaving the *China Queen* with the same frantic urgency of rats abandoning a sinking ship. Only a few members of the crew were remaining with the captain. A few were straining on the capstan as they brought up the anchor, while others were clambering up the rigging to unfurl the sails. It was obvious that Captain Sutherland was anxious to put this unlucky landfall behind him.

Meanwhile, Hawk commandeered a lifeboat. Nat and Sam lowered it, while Hawk waited above them on deck for Marta and Bannister to come topside. He was about ready to go down after them when Marta appeared on deck. She stumbled as she ran across the unlit deck toward him.

"Martin's got another gun!" she cried. "He says he's coming after you. He swears he won't leave this ship."

"The hell with him, then," Hawk barked. "Get into the lifeboat!"

Taking Marta by the arm, Hawk helped her down the rope ladder, then jumped into the boat after her. Snatching up an oar, he fitted it into an oarlock.

"Pull away," he told Nat and Sam. "Hurry!"

As he pulled hard on his oar, Hawk glanced back at the ship. Bannister was leaning over the ship's rail, a gun in his hand. Lifting it, he aimed quickly and fired. The round sent a geyser of water into the air a few feet ahead of the lifeboat.

Hawk was about to ship his oar and return Bannister's fire when members of the crew caught him from behind. Bannister struggled for a moment, then vanished. Then came a flurry of shots. Hawk heard shouts from the captain, followed by oaths and more shooting.

"Look!" said Sam, pointing.

The *China Queen*'s recently unfurled sails were billowing as a sudden, unexpected wind filled them. The graceful bow of the clipper ship dipped, its prow slicing through the waves as the ship started to make for a rocky headland that stretched almost halfway across the cove's entrance.

With surprising speed, the ship neared the headland. Shots sounded dimly from the ship. Hawk thought he could hear the captain's strident, desperate voice as he issued orders to his small crew. One, then two sailors dived overboard. Closer and closer the ship drew to the menacing headland.

"There's no one at the helm," Sam said, his voice hushed.

Fire erupted from the ship's bow. With ravening speed, it swept out of the forecastle and surged across the main deck, then leapt eagerly up a mast. With an explosion they could hear even at this distance, one entire sail was transformed into a sheet of flame.

A second later the ship's bow rose slightly out of the water as it struck the headland and with an almost perverse momentum continued to grind relentlessly up onto the rocks. Meanwhile, the water around the ship became as bright as day as the fire swept through it, the flames leaping as high as the topmost mast, devouring sails furled and unfurled.

"I don't think the captain or Bannister had a chance to escape," said Nat.

"Neither do I," agreed Hawk.

"It was such a beautiful ship," Marta murmured.

"No, Marta, it wasn't," Sam told her. "It was a devil ship. Everyone said so, and they were right."

"Yes," agreed Nat. "A ship is more than wood and sail. It has a soul, I think. Or at least it should have. This one's soul was in the service of the devil."

They placed their oars back into the water and pulled for shore.

Glancing back over his shoulder as he rowed, Hawk saw Tames Horses and Mary Jane standing on the beach, holding the bridles of their saddled horses. He guided the lifeboat toward them.

On a knoll overlooking the Pacific, Hawk and Tames Horses sat astride their mounts. Below them, heading down a well-traveled trail that would take them to California and the goldfields, Mary Jane and Nat Carlson turned in their saddles and waved good-bye to Hawk and Tames Horses. Mounted just behind them, Sam and Marta also waved. Marta had had a difficult time these past two weeks. Her habit had been a strong one, but she was on the mend now, and with Mary Jane to help her through it, there was no doubt in Hawk's mind that Marta would lick her addiction.

A moment later the four riders vanished from sight as the trail dipped below a foothill.

Though Hawk knew Tames Horses would never admit it, the Indian had hoped that Mary Jane would return to the mountains with him. Nevertheless, he had shown no emotion when Mary Jane announced her intention to ride on down to California with Nat and to take Sam and Marta with them.

It was a solution Hawk applauded, and Tames Horses could see at once the wisdom of this choice. But now, the look in his eyes as he watched Mary Jane disappear from view was a little like watching the sun go down.

And for Tames Horses, it was. For the last time a fire was going out inside him, one Mary Jane had rekindled.

Tames Horses spoke suddenly. "I do not want Mary Jane to find gold. If she does, it will make her crazy."

"What makes you say that, Chief?"

"Gold always drive white people crazy."

"You're right, Tames Horses. It does at that."

Hawk pulled his horse around and headed east toward the beckoning rampart of mountains. Tames Horses did likewise and kept alongside Hawk as they rode.

"I wouldn't worry none," Hawk told the chief. "I don't think she's going to spend much time looking for gold. I figure she'll settle down with Nat and have children. That one of yours first, of course."

Tames Horses glanced quickly at Hawk. "You know of this?"

"Last night Mary Jane told me. She's a very proud woman, Tames Horses. She says it will be a son—a very brave son. She says she will call him Bright Path, and she is certain he will stand up to his enemies and never shame her—or your memory."

Tames Horses straightened proudly in his saddle. "Yes. It will be fine son," he said.

They said no more about it. The matter was closed, and Hawk rode on, well pleased. He had found Sam and Marta. His long search for them was over. Bannister had been stopped. As for Tames Horses, the old warrior had bathed in the Pacific as had no other Nez Percé in his band, and he had quite possibly sired a new offspring. If he could never know this for sure, it didn't matter. A man couldn't always know the truth of such things.

And now Hawk was returning to the mountains and the Snake River Valley in the company of an old and trusted friend. He was content.